The Spanish Acquisition

Nora Snowdon

CRIMSON
ROMANCE
F+W Media, Inc.

Published by
Crimson Romance
an imprint of F+W Media, Inc.
10151 Carver Road, Suite 200
Blue Ash, Ohio 45242

www.crimsonromance.com

ISBN 10: 1-4405-5997-X
ISBN 13: 978-1-4405-5997-6
eISBN 10: 1-4405-5998-8
eISBN 13: 978-1-4405-5998-3

Chapter One

Inhaling the soothing scent of fresh hay and horses, Carlos Diego let the tension of the last few weeks seep from his jet-lagged limbs. It was good to be back among honest friends. A horse would always treat you fairly, unlike many people. He scowled, the environmentalists protesting his ship's recovery never far from his mind these days. Would they rather he left it littering the ocean floor? Still, Carlos's absence would send a clear message that he would not be intimidated. And his legal team was standing by. As he neared the stalls, several horses popped their heads over the doors to greet him. A large chestnut whinnied hopefully.

"*Para usted, mi amigo…*" he murmured, watching the horse eagerly chomp on the carrot sticks he'd taken from the buffet table. A rub on the nose and then he went in search of his favorite mount. "*Buenas tardes, muchacho.*" The bay gelding reached over his gate to nuzzle Carlos's shirt. "You remember me from last year. Or maybe you smell the treat?"

A feminine squeak and a loud thump made him turn and take a step toward the other side of the stalls. A young woman was awkwardly getting up from the ground. Her strange attire of baggy cargo shorts, an old rock t-shirt, and cheap high-top sneakers made him wonder if she'd snuck in from a less exclusive hotel down the beach.

"Are you all right?" Carlos extended a hand to help her to her feet. Upon closer inspection, he realized she wasn't as young as he first suspected—her fingers were calloused and she definitely was an adult. Her eyes, when she finally looked up at him, were a striking shade of blue set against porcelain skin that was quickly turning red. This was a person who would have a difficult time lying, he decided.

"Oh, I—I'm fine," the woman stammered. "I, um, was just patting the horse, and it suddenly jerked its head up. I was startled, that's all."

"It looks like you scared the horse as well." Carlos approached the gray and quietly blew into its nostrils. The mare calmed down immediately. "Would you like to give her a treat?" He gave a carrot stick to the woman and she offered it nervously to the horse. "Hold it out with a flat palm," he advised.

"Her mouth feels so soft." Her eyes widened with amazement. "Can I give her another one?"

"Just one more. We do not want to spoil her figure," he teased.

This time her hand was steady. She really was beautiful. Jet black hair framed a sweet, heart-shaped face. Her lips, although unadorned by any makeup, seemed plump and inviting. What he could see of her figure looked entrancing. A pleasant change from the usual array of Botox, silicone, and surgery-enhanced women he usually encountered at the resort.

"Now you have a friend for life. Have you signed up for a trail ride?" Carlos wasn't sure why he cared if she was sneaking into the resort. She didn't seem intent on mischief, but he was curious.

"Maybe tomorrow. I just got here. I figured I'd meet the horses first and then see how you go about getting to ride them. Do you work here?"

"No." He stifled a smile at the thought. "I am a guest."

"Oh, sorry. You look so comfortable around the horses."

"Ah *si*, horses are my family. But where are my manners? I am Carlos Diego, at your service." He bowed low and lightly kissed the back of her hand. Her flustered response amused him.

"Oh, pleased to meet cha. I'm Lily Scott."

"Your name sounds familiar. Should I know you from film or music?"

"I don't think so." She laughed. "I was once employee of the month at the Mac's in Springfield, Oregon, but that was ten years ago. Well, I'd better go. Nice meeting you."

She'd turned away before Carlos realized that she had assumed his question had been a pick-up line. And she had rebuffed him. How unusual. But her name did ring a bell and he was never mistaken on names.

"*Uno momento*. Do you have plans for dinner tonight, or are you here with your husband?"

"I'm not married."

"Good. Then you will meet me at seven at The Captain's Table?" he challenged her. If nothing else, it would be interesting to see what she wore to dinner. A variety of thoughts flitted across her face before she came to a decision.

"Okay, sure." She rubbed her palm on the side of her shorts. "That's one of the restaurants in this resort, right?"

"*Si*. The food is very good."

"Great. I guess I'll see you later."

Carlos admired her shapely legs as she hurried out of the barn. He obviously made her nervous but she had agreed to dine with him. Quite an interesting mixture of shyness and determination. If he didn't remember soon where he recognized her name, he would ask his assistant. But meanwhile she might be a nice diversion.

*

Negative. The undisputable truth. Carlos stood in his luxury suite and turned over the single sheet of fax paper. Incredible that such a small physical item could have such an impact on his life. He read the report from the lab one more time. His anger built as he recalled Elena's tearful speech all those months ago.

"No, of course there has been no one else. I love only you. We must've used a faulty condom." Luckily, Carlos had heeded his lawyer's advice about waiting to marry her until after the DNA test came back. Why was he such a fool? He'd even been happy at the thought of having a baby.

Carlos balled up the page and flung it into the garbage can. He would not be fooled again. Elena was a beautiful, if somewhat greedy woman, but he hadn't thought she was so deceptive. Would she now try to pawn the baby off on some other billionaire? And how many others was she sleeping with? He ground his teeth as he e-mailed instructions to his personal lawyer. Elena had crossed the wrong man. She'd pay dearly for that mistake.

*

"Aunt Lilith, this place is incredible. The suite is huge with a Jacuzzi and a sauna. And you should see the beach. The water is so clear you can see to the bottom even when you're in way over your head. This is like a dream come true." Lily flopped back on the giant bed and switched the phone to her other ear so she could gaze out the window. "I can't thank you enough for giving me this trip."

"Oh, forget about it. The ticket was a freebie. I think that company gave it to me so I wouldn't sue them after falling in their gallery. Lawrence was disgusted I wouldn't let him take them to court. You know, I never would've encouraged law school if I'd known he would end up so greedy like his father."

"But I thought you tripped because your heel broke."

"Lawrence says that doesn't matter. Big companies will pay to avoid press. But it's a moot point. I ain't suing, and you're getting a vacation in the Dominican Republic out of the deal. But if you want to bring me something back…"

"Sure, anything."

"Well I've always wanted my own cabana boy." Lilith's raucous laugh devolved into her smoker's hack.

"I'll see what I can do." Lily smiled. "Oh and guess what else? This handsome guy asked me to dinner. And I said yes. Are you proud of me?"

"Hmm. Very. But make sure you use protection."

"Aunt Lilith! He just asked me to dinner. I'm not going to sleep with him."

"Why not? You're young, available. Now if I were twenty-seven… "

"I don't even know him." Lily couldn't believe they were discussing this. "Besides, then I'd have to list it the next time I gave blood."

"You need to loosen up, Lily. Sex can be fun."

"I know, I know, Aunt Lilith." God, she wished she'd never told her aunt about Danny. "Look I'd better go. This call is costing you a bundle. Thanks again for the trip. I love you."

Lily hung up and hugged a big pillow to her chest. She wasn't going to worry about dinner tonight. It would be fun and, since the guy—Carlos, wasn't it? Oh God, was that his name?—wasn't paying for her meal, he couldn't expect her to sleep with him. Despite her aunt's preoccupation, not everyone was having non-stop sex.

*

Lily flipped through the brochures on her night table to see how dressed up she should be for The Captain's Table. Of course, she grumbled, everyone in brochures was dressed to the nines. Then again, was this considered a date? It wasn't as though he had to pick her up, pay for her, or anything. Still there might be a dress code. Aunt Lilith had insisted she pack some fancy clothes just in case. "You don't want to be schlepping about in your glad rags. It's all well and good to dress like a homeless bum around the art school, but you'll meet classier people if you try to dress like one."

Yet she'd met Carlos—yes, that was his name—in her "glad rags." She should've told Aunt Lilith that. Lily chose her blue wrap dress as it was pretty without being too revealing. Then she washed and pinned her hair up on top of her head with a few curly tendrils framing her face. Tremors of excitement danced through her as she applied her lip gloss. She considered nylons, but couldn't bear to put them on in this heat. Carlos would have to put up with her shockingly white legs. With a little luck, she might be slightly darker by the end of her vacation, but even that wasn't a sure thing.

Mostly she didn't care how she looked, but for some reason the concept of dinner with this man made her feel incredibly unsophisticated. In their brief encounter, he'd seemed so suave. It wasn't that he was older—he appeared close to her age—but he was unnervingly confident. She had debated several times whether to call him to cancel their dinner but couldn't think of a good excuse. And it wasn't like she wanted to eat alone. But what if he was a weirdo? At home in New York, she'd never let a pushy stranger take her out.

It was almost seven. Was Carlos a punctual person? She hated being the first one at a restaurant. Her friends would say she should arrive a little late, to be stylish. Or was it to make him think she wasn't too eager? She couldn't remember. It might be out of her hands anyway—she wasn't sure where The Captain's Table was. She had passed a number of restaurants and dining rooms in her first run around the resort. If it was that expensive one with the dark wood and snotty looking servers, then it was easy to get to. That restaurant had looked sort of nautical, so she'd try it first.

She was just nearing the paneled doors when Carlos stepped out from beside the floral decor.

"*Ah bella,* you are on time. Good." Carlos kissed her hand, then leaned back to assess her. "You are very beautiful."

"Thank you." It was probably a European thing, but the way his eyes swept her from head to toe was intimate and embarrassing. Plus he was even more attractive than she recalled. His face had that tanned, chiseled look of a professional model. Except that perhaps his nose was a tad more generous. And his dark curly hair failed to conceal a faint scar on his temple. But other than that—

"Was the rest of your afternoon entertaining?"

"Yeah, I checked out the beach and the pool. There are whirlpools built right into the pool. How do they fix them when they break?"

"It's not something I've ever worried about."

"I guess not. Oh, and there's a swim up bar, too." *Oh God, I'm rambling on like a small town hick. Shut up!*

"*Si.* I have stayed here before." His slow smile revealed perfect teeth. *Of course.*

The maître d' appeared with a silent grace. "Your table is right this way, *Señor* Diego."

Carlos placed his hand on the small of her back and directed her forward. Lily jumped at the shock wave his casual touch sent through her body. She almost stepped on the maître d's heels in her attempt to distance herself from the contact.

"What is it you do in Springfield, Lily?" Carlos asked after they were seated.

"Oh, I live in New York now. I'm an artist." She suddenly felt embarrassed. What if he asked her where she had shown? He probably only considered people who sold their stuff for millions to be artists.

"It is a difficult profession, no?"

"Well I'm actually a massage therapist as well. That helps to cover the bills." His eyes lit up at the word massage and she inwardly groaned. Why did some guys assume massage is some kind of code for prostitution?

"I see."

Lily was relieved when the waiter interrupted.

"Would you like to start off with something to drink?"

"A lemonade for me, please. And a glass of water." Should she have specified bottled water, or was the tap water safe? Oh well, she'd see what they brought.

"A bottle of your Sauvignon Blanc, *gracias.* You will join me in a taste?"

"No thank you. I don't drink."

"You don't drink anything?" Carlos gave her a look of disbelief.

"Not alcohol." Lily hated feeling defensive about not drinking. She never bothered people if they didn't like chocolate. He seemed to be waiting for a reason so she added lamely, "Hey, don't let me stop you."

"Thank you. You do realize that in Spain you might be hanged for a witch, for such odd behavior?"

"I'll try to remember not to go there. So what's good here?"

"Perhaps you will allow me to order for you?"

"If you promise to avoid jellyfish and snails, then sure."

"Certainly." With a discreet nod from Carlos, the waiter quickly reappeared. Carlos discussed several options with him until they came to a mutually agreeably decision. The waiter withdrew.

"That all sounds wonderful, but do you think we can eat that much?" Lily asked tentatively.

"Well, if you aren't drinking, we must find another way to excite your palate."

"As long as I don't get too heavy to ride a horse tomorrow," she joked. "I've never ridden and it's been a goal of mine forever."

"Really? And why have you never done this?"

"Because it's expensive." Was he making fun of her?

"Oh." Carlos sounded surprised. "I will go with you tomorrow. The first group goes out at ten o'clock."

"No! I mean…" She scrambled to think of an excuse. "I'll probably be very slow and it'll be boring for you." Despite herself, Lily almost hoped he'd override her objections. What was wrong with her? She wasn't even sure that she liked him, but she was mesmerized by his seductive smile.

"It is a beautiful ride along the beach. I can think of no one I would rather be with. Would you like me to order a slow horse for you?"

"I don't know. I like going fast on bikes, but…" Lily chewed on her bottom lip while she thought about it. "No. I think I'd like a fast horse. Either you fall or you don't, it probably doesn't make much difference how fast you go." The waiter reappeared with several plates of appetizers, which Lily eyed with a mixture of apprehension and delight. "Wow. I sure hope you're hungry."

"Ravenous." Carlos's sensuous smile kicked up a notch, and Lily's breath caught in surprise. It seemed he could turn on the sexual heat at will. "Try one of these." He held a prawn up to her lips.

Lily carefully took his offering with her fingers and popped it in her mouth. She ignored his teasing look. "Mmm, that is good." She pointed at an odd looking deep-fried dish. "But what's this?"

"It is the conch fritter. Don't worry, I did not order anything scary." Carlos helped himself to a selection of each of the dishes. "Unless you do not approve of blow fish?"

"What's that?" Lily eyed him suspiciously.

"A specialty that is very popular in Japan. It is delicious, but if it is not prepared correctly, it will kill you instantly."

"What!" Lily looked with horror at the dishes on the table.

"I did not order it. They do not even have it here." Carlos raised her hand up to his lips. "You can trust me."

Lily's heart raced at his unexpected gesture. Maybe she could trust him, but could she trust herself? He had a way of focusing his intense gaze on her that made her quiver inside. This was ridiculous. She didn't even know the man. Self-consciously, she pulled her hand away. "So you're saying that nothing here will kill me. Well, that's a relief. Playing Russian roulette with food never struck me as a good idea."

*

Carlos sipped his wine and considered the chameleon across the table. She wasn't adding up to be the person he'd assumed. Or else she was a damn good actress. She seemed very naïve and genuine.

And she certainly cleaned up beautifully from her earlier ruffian look. But surely if she worked in one of those sleazy massage parlors, she wouldn't be so quick to blush at his every move on her. Either way, she was a delightful puzzle for him to play with while he was here.

He watched her cautiously eat a conch fritter, admiring her beautiful bow lips closing around her fork. He wanted to kiss those lips and feel their softness against his. She blushed and Carlos realized he was staring. Again. *Dios*, but it was difficult to think about food around this woman. Carlos refilled his wine while he considered his next move. He decided to tackle the question head on.

"So, why did you get into massage as a profession?"

"It's a long story." She shrugged dismissively.

Carlos sat back in his chair. "I'd love to hear it."

She paused as if contemplating how much to say. "I guess it was about ten years ago. My mother had been very sick for a year and, well, the doctors were competent, but they seemed to treat her like a bunch of symptoms and ailments, you know, not like a real person."

She hesitated again and Carlos nodded in encouragement.

"Well, near the end of her life, we had this marvelous guy from the Home Care Agency. He was a massage therapist. I mean, he couldn't cure her, but he helped her feel a lot better. Some of what he did was just listening to her and validating her feelings. After Mom died, my aunt suggested I move to New York to study art. I did, but I also attended massage school so I could be like that caregiver and help people. It was a bit tight at first, but now that I've got regular customers, it's actually a good profession."

"But don't you have to worry about strange customers?"

"I'm very picky and only take people who are referred to me. Early on I had a stalker client. That was scary. After that I started asking for references."

"What did he do?"

"No, it was a she. And it was mostly that she kept turning up everywhere, phoning at all hours, and leaving me odd little notes. I still don't know how she knew my every move, but it was unnerving."

"How did you stop her?"

"I threatened to go to the cops, but I think she must have moved away, gotten locked up, or something. I changed my phone number, but nowadays with the internet, if someone wants to find you, it's not that difficult."

"That is true. So you only massage people who are ill?" He kept the skepticism from his voice.

"Well, some are sick. I treat this one woman with torticollis. For some reason her neck muscles pull her head to always look to the left. I can't cure it, but I work on the other muscles that are pulling against the neck muscles. Other people come for general stiffness or sports injuries."

"Don't you need medical training for that?"

"It was an intense two-year course with lots of anatomy and biology." She sounded defensive.

He nodded. "That is impressive."

"Yeah. So that's enough about me. What about you? You're from Spain?"

"*Si*, Barcelona. I have one sister, and my mother is still there." Carlos shifted his wine glass to make room for the waiter to put down their main course of lobster, baked potato, and melted butter.

"Oh my God. What is that?" Lily's eyes widened in alarm.

"Lobster. You have not eaten it before?"

"No..." She paused and reconsidered. "Well, actually, I guess I have. A friend used to make fancy party sandwiches with canned lobster paste and pickles. This doesn't look quite like that." She poked the lobster shell with her fingertip. "Hmm, how do you eat it?"

"Here, allow me." Carlos reached across and cracked open her lobster. He speared a piece with his lobster fork, dipped it in the melted butter, and offered it to her with a smile. She hesitated only slightly before leaning forward to taste the shellfish.

"Wow. That is way better than the canned stuff." She smiled sheepishly at him. "But do you mind—?" Lily put a cloth napkin over the lobster's head. "There's something wrong with being watched by your dinner."

Carlos laughed. "You don't eat fish, either?"

"Not with the heads on." Her nose crinkled in disgust. "I mostly cook pasta at home. But I want to try lots of different foods on vacation. Then again, maybe I should stick to lobster every night." They wrestled with the lobsters in companionable silence for a while before Lily asked, "Is lobster fattening?"

"We'll ride tomorrow then, in case you get too big to go later on," Carlos teased. He speared another choice piece of lobster and held it out to her. "Here, this is a good part." He watched her luscious mouth close around the morsel and then her eyes shut as she savored the taste.

"Mmm. That was so good, but I can't eat another bite. Can we get a doggy bag?" she asked with a smile.

"No. But don't worry. There will be more food tomorrow." He signaled to the waiter. "May I interest you in some dessert and coffee?"

"I can't believe I'm saying this, but I'm too full for dessert. Hey, it's almost time for the evening show. Do you think they'll let us take our coffee in the theater?"

"Certainly. But you want to see that?" Carlos asked surprised.

"Yeah. Don't you?"

"Of course," he answered swiftly with a smile. "You realize it will not be like the excellent shows you see in New York?"

"I haven't been to many shows in New York. I go to several art exhibits a month—if they're free. And a few years ago a friend from school had tickets to *Movin' Out*, the Billy Joel musical. Other than that…"

"Let's watch this one then, and we can see how it compares to Billy Joel."

*

They settled into the theater chairs early because Lily wanted to make sure they got in. Now looking at all the vacant seats, she understood why Carlos hadn't been too concerned. Still they got good seats and, since they weren't in the front, no one would use them in their act. She'd been to a comedy club in SoHo once, and the comedian had picked on the people in the front row. It was unpleasant to watch and it must've been twice as bad for those poor people.

She glanced around with curiosity. It was a small theater with crimson red velvet curtains and matching fabric on the walls. The seats even had little cup holders like the ones at the movies.

"This is so cool," Lily whispered to Carlos when the lights dimmed.

He smiled and stretched his arm out along the back of her chair. There was a loud percussion, and then the band—she looked to see where they were playing, but couldn't see them—started up with "Let Me Entertain You." One long leg in a very high heel kicked out from behind the curtain. Then it was followed by one gorgeous, long-legged beauty after another, doing a Ziegfeld Follies routine.

"They're beautiful," Lily said in awe. "I bet they can't eat lobster every night and keep those figures."

"Probably not," Carlos whispered back. "But I think a lot of their looks are achieved in the doctor's office."

"Doctors can't make your legs that long," she countered.

"True. But look at the heels they are wearing."

"Wearing those is a skill all on its own." Carlos laughed and Lily turned away from the stage to look up at him. "It's true. Mere mortals would fall over."

He pulled her closer and asked, "And what do you think of the singing?"

"The brunette in red has a good voice, but the others …" Lily paused, trying to think of a polite way to say it. "Well, they're mostly on tune, but not that good."

It felt good to have his arm around her shoulders. Comfortable, she realized. When he whispered in her ear, a shiver shot down her spine.

"And the dancing?" His breath tickled.

"That's not their fault. That's crappy choreography. Even I could follow those dance steps." Lily chuckled. "Well, not in those shoes."

The name of the revue was *Broadway Lights* and followed a loose plot involving a sweet girl named Babs trying to get into a Broadway revue. A lot of songs from *42nd Street* fit easily, but it was a bit of a stretch when Babs sang the main song from *Cats*. The big boffo ending was the entire cast singing "Just One Night" from *Dreamgirls* as Babs took over for the evil lead actress with the broken leg. Lily applauded enthusiastically until every performer had left the stage.

"Did you really enjoy it that much?" he asked.

"No. But did you see how much some of those performers were sweating? They were working hard. And it would be difficult doing that every night. Wouldn't it be fun if one night the bad girl said at the end, 'You know, I think my leg isn't broken after all,' and see how the other performers worked around that?"

"I hope you do not plan on seeing the show every night in case she does."

"No. I bet they've got pretty good contracts to keep them from doing it. But you'd want to."

"It is still early. Would you like to go to one of the nightclubs?" he asked.

"Sorry, but I think I'm going to call it a night. I've been so excited about this trip that I haven't slept for several days now. And I want to be alert and ready for horseback riding tomorrow. Where and when should I meet you?"

"Quarter to ten at the concierge desk. Or meet me for breakfast at nine, if you're awake." Carlos paused and then added, "I'll walk you up to your room, now."

"Um, sure." Lily was both thrilled and nervous at the way his arm curled protectively around her waist. She wondered again if he considered this a date and if he'd expect a goodnight kiss. Or was he hoping she'd invite him in for a nightcap? Since she didn't drink, it seemed unlikely. She tried not to worry about it. She'd find out soon enough when they got to her door.

She paused to sniff at one of the large orange flowers lining the walkway back to the hotel. She frowned and Carlos smiled at her puzzled look.

"That is bougainvillea. It has no scent but it is very beautiful, *si*?"

"Yeah. It still seems strange coming from the cold winter in New York to this. It's going to be hard to go back next week."

"You have only arrived. It is too soon to be worried about returning." He picked a bloom and tucked it into her hair. In the elevator, she watched the floor numbers go by and desperately tried to think of something witty to say.

When they finally reached her room she turned to Carlos with a smile. "Well, this is me. Thank you. That was a fun dinner and show. I'll see you tomorrow, probably at breakfast." Before she could turn back to her door, Carlos had pulled her gently into his arms. She watched his lips descending slowly to hers. She could duck away. Instead she closed her eyes.

His lips were gentle at first, but then his hand held her head closer and his mouth demanded more. Lily gasped as his tongue slid in to explore her mouth. It was a strange and thrilling sensation. He seemed to consume her with his need. And her body responded far quicker than her mind. Her hands reached up to run through his hair and her body pressed closer against his.

Through the pounding of her own heartbeat, she barely heard his groan when she kissed the pulse at the side of his neck. He even tasted good. His hand ran down her backside and drew her leg up to curl around his outer thigh. She felt his teeth nibble lightly on her ear sending chills running down her spine. Suddenly his hand touched the side of her breast and she pulled away with a start.

"Excuse me. I'd better get to bed. I, I mean—" Lily fumbled for the card to unlock her door.

"Certainly. I shall see you tomorrow morning. *Buenas nochas.*" Carlos kissed her cheek and stroked her hair before she ducked into the safety of her room.

Once inside, Lily leaned against the back of her door and slid down it in shock. She'd only met this guy today, and here she was making out with him in the hallway! What was wrong with her? Yes, he was gorgeous and seemed very nice. And he smelled heavenly, too. But he could be a whacko for all she knew. Or married. To top it off, he lived in another country, so there was no hope of a real relationship. She would not let herself be used by a man, she resolved, no matter how much she wanted him.

She sighed involuntarily, her body still quivering from the heat of his caresses. Now she just had to figure out how to backtrack with him. She had a feeling it wasn't going to be easy.

*

Carlos strode back to his suite in confusion. He'd been sure from her enthusiastic response to his kiss that she would invite him into her room. Her reaction at the end had been that of an inexperienced teenager, but she was certainly older than that. He tried to recall if she'd mentioned her age. She'd been working ten years ago so she was at least twenty-five. At most, six years younger than him. No *Americana* would remain a virgin at that age. And her responses up until she stopped him had definitely been that of a woman. He gritted his teeth recalling her gentle love bites on his neck. A cold shower tonight or he'd never get to sleep. But first he would see if he had any communications from his office.

As he read the e-mail from his personal assistant, Carlos smiled incredulously. What were the odds? Lilith Scott was the woman who had fallen at the Klee exhibit his company was touring. His new assistant had stupidly given the woman that bitch Elena's unused vacation after she had backed out last minute for a photo shoot. He'd almost fired the girl for that. Americans were litigious enough without encouraging their greed. Now having met Ms. Scott, he felt fairly certain she wouldn't take his company to court. Obviously she was not grievously wounded. To be safe he would keep this revelation to himself. After Elena's deception, he would not let himself be fooled again. But getting closer to Ms. Scott would be an amusing way to determine her intentions.

Chapter Two

A warm tropical breeze greeted Lily as she admired the view from her spacious balcony. The sound of children playing drifted up from the pool and she tried to guess what language they were speaking. After a few moments she gave up and instead turned her attention to the vibrant colors of the windsurfers getting an early start on the day's activities. Maybe after riding she'd take her watercolors to the beach and try to catch their essence. Or she could try sketching the horses. Or the children. Man, this was the life.

With a start Lily realized she'd better get cracking. She'd slept in later than she'd planned. No surprise there. She'd tossed and turned in her huge bed for ages, reliving each touch, word, and sensual look that Carlos had given her. Then she fell into such a heavy sleep that she could barely open her eyes at eight o'clock. She had been dreaming of Carlos…which was allowed as long as it was only a dream.

Lily showered and dressed in jeans and a t-shirt. She was nervous about seeing him again. Would he think she was a tease for the way she'd behaved the night before? Or just very immature? He was so sophisticated, he probably had women lining up to jump in bed with him. And from the way he kissed, he probably would be very good there. Her mind still reeled. But how would she feel afterward if she gave in to her desires? She tied her hair back, put on sun block, a little eyeliner, and headed down to breakfast.

Lily's stomach was fluttering long before she saw him. When she spotted him casually dressed in jeans and a pale button-down shirt, her stomach switched into cartwheels. Could she quickly run back to her room to steady her nerves? He waved to her. Her escape was too slow. She forced a smile and sat down at his table.

"*Buenos días.*"

"Morning. Looks like a beautiful day for horseback riding."

"How about some breakfast first?" Carlos suggested with a smile.

Lily checked out all the breakfast options on the buffet table and then filled up a plate with fruit.

"Is that all you are eating?" He looked from her plate to the eggs and waffles stacked on his.

"I love fresh fruit. Imagine if you could get up every day to a breakfast feast like this. I wish I could move in here."

"Just for the food?"

"Everything else is pretty amazing, too." She laughed, embarrassed. "I guess you're used to this luxury."

"Because?" His eyes narrowed.

"Well, you've been here before. Didn't you say that?"

"Yes, of course." A corner of his mouth lifted in an amused smile. Had she missed something?

She bit into a slice of pineapple then quickly caught the juice before it ran down her chin. *Smaller pieces and use your knife and fork. But what about the watermelon pits?* Darn, she should've gone for less socially challenging food. She daintily cut up the honeydew slices. He appeared unconcerned as he dug into his food.

"So, I'm finally going to ride a horse." Lily chewed on her lower lip.

"Are you nervous?"

"Yeah, a little. It's been a dream of mine for so long, you know. When I was young, I read *Black Beauty, The Black Stallion, My Friend Flicka*, all those horse books, and I guess horses became an escape for me. Now I wonder if it'll be a letdown, actually being on one."

His fork paused midway to his mouth. "What were you escaping?"

Lily glanced away before answering, "You know, childhood things." She turned back to him. "Can we go hang out with the horses again before we ride them?"

"Certainly. May I finish my coffee before we go?"

"Only if you hurry," she advised him.

*

Standing outside the stable, waiting for their horses to be brought out, Lily wiped her hands on her jeans. Paul, the trail guide, had given them all tips on how to behave around the horses. He seemed especially concerned about keeping the two rowdy German teenagers in line. He reiterated that one good blow from a horse's hoof could kill a man. Lily was suitably scared but the boys continued roughhousing. He gave the duo another stern look before he went into the barn to retrieve her gray and the bay for Carlos. When he returned he looped their reins around the fence and then went back for the horses for the two kids, who were busy making bets on who could ride faster.

"Wow. She's even more beautiful in the sunlight." Lily tentatively approached the dappled gray mare. "Hey, Quicksilver." She showed her hand slowly to the horse before reaching out to pat her neck as Paul had suggested. "She seems a lot bigger. How do I get up there?"

"First lesson, you always have to mount the horse from the left side."

"Always? Even in Australia?"

"Yes, even in Australia. Here I will give you a lift." Carlos boosted her into the saddle. Lily sat uneasily while Carlos adjusted her stirrups. It was way higher than she had realized. Her horse wasn't even moving and she felt wobbly.

Carlos continued, "Now, when you want the horse to turn to the left, you pull on the left rein. The right turns her the other way. And if you want her to slow down or stop, you pull back on both reins."

Lily tugged back experimentally.

"Whoa!" Carlos jumped out of the way as her horse began backing up. Lily gasped and grabbed the saddle horn.

"Unless you are standing still, then pulling back on the reins tells the horse to back up," Carlos explained as he took control of the leather straps. "Now, hold the reins not so strong. That's good." He quickly mounted his own horse. "Hold tight with your knees. And when you are ready to go, a kick to the belly tells the horse to go forward. You are comfortable?"

"I guess so. I feel a little unsteady," she admitted.

"That is fine. We will follow Paul and the other riders and walk for the first bit, until you get used to it," Carlos reassured her. "What is it you Americans say, 'It's easy, just like falling off a bicycle'?"

Her horse automatically followed the others and Lily felt a little better. She didn't like the idea of kicking the poor animal. She tried turning her horse by pulling on one rein, but it didn't seem inclined to obey; it just followed the horse in front. She smiled back at Carlos as they rode along the pathway. At this speed she felt okay. They reached a grassy area and Paul turned back to shout.

"You can gallop your horses here. If you don't want to, hold back on the reins until the rest have gotten ahead."

Carlos looked over at Lily. "Would you like to try trotting first?"

"Yup."

He reached over and held her horse while the others galloped off.

"Hug the horse with your knees and hold on to the horn if you want." Carlos lightly swatted her horse on the butt, and then urged his own into a trot.

It felt very awkward as she bounced up and down on the hard saddle. A couple of times she landed too close to the horn and that was even worse. They went in a small circle.

"You are doing very well," Carlos called out over the bumping and squeaking noises of their horses and saddles. "Are you ready to try a little faster?"

"I guess so." Lily had only a small tremor in her voice.

"Just lean forward and try to move with your horse. Don't fight it." He leaned over and gave her horse another tap on the butt.

Quicksilver's gait changed into a faster, but much less bumpy stride. Lily tried leaning forward just as Quicksilver's head rocked backwards and she narrowly avoided colliding with its neck. She grimaced as she grabbed on to the saddle horn yet again.

"Feel your mount's rhythm," Carlos hollered. "It is like dancing with a partner."

With grim determination, Lily let herself be lulled into Quicksilver's motion. It was like a rocking horse, she finally realized with a giggle. As long as she didn't fight the movement, it was quite smooth. She laughed out loud when Carlos cantered by and turned to head down toward the beach. She leaned a little to the right in her saddle as she pulled on the one rein. Quicksilver turned as she was asked and Lily felt oddly proud.

Then when they straightened out to run along the beach, Lily sensed that something was wrong. Her saddle seemed to be still tilting to the right. She tried to correct it by leaning left, but somehow the whole saddle kept shifting the other way with her in it. She pulled on the reins to stop Quicksilver. The horse ignored her, intent on catching up to Carlos's mount.

This is silly. She tried to keep from panicking. *Maybe I just need to turn the other way.* But the horse wasn't listening to her as she yanked on the reins with increasing strength. The saddle slid further down the horse's belly. She let out a cry of shock when Quicksilver's hoof connected with her calf. The horse stumbled slightly and pain shot through Lily's leg. Her fear seemed to slow down time. Her right foot was flopping under the horse's stomach, but the horse kept running.

"Carlos!" she screamed. The hooves were flying ever closer to her head. She couldn't think about Paul's earlier comment. She tried to climb up the saddle, which was now halfway under the belly, but her feet were trapped in her stirrups. *Am I going to die?* "Help!" she managed to eek out. Her brain was racing in all directions. Could she somehow throw herself clear of the horse without getting trampled to death?

"Grab the horse's mane!" Carlos commanded.

Oh God, yes! She grabbed a handful of horsehair and pulled herself slightly away from the terrifying hooves. Suddenly a hand looped under her armpit and started to lift her up. Her mind went blank as she felt herself being torn in two directions.

"Let go, Lily! I've got you."

She couldn't understand what he meant until she realized that her hand was still in a death grip with the poor horse's mane. She quickly let go and felt a jolt, her body slamming against Carlos's horse. Another hand secured her and then she was lifted up onto the other horse. She grabbed Carlos's neck and buried her face in his shoulder. She heard him say something, but didn't know what. She closed her eyes, trying to make the fear go away.

*

"Lily! Are you all right? *¡Dios!*" Carlos reined his horse to a stop and attempted to pry Lily away from his neck so he could make sure she wasn't hurt. She wouldn't budge so he gave up and patted her ineffectually on her shaking shoulders. "It is all right. You are safe now. Lily?" He kissed the top of her head and murmured again, "I have you. You are safe. It's all right, *bella*." He'd never felt so helpless. She didn't seem to hear him at all. Then she murmured something into his neck. "*¿Qué?* I cannot hear you, Lily."

"I shouldn't have leaned," she whimpered. "On motorcycles you have to lean to turn. I didn't know—"

"Oh no, *bella*. That was not your fault. They didn't—"

"Did I hurt the horse? I didn't mean to." She lifted her head and searched frantically for her horse.

"She is fine. See over there? I think she is going back to her barn."

There was a thunder of hooves and Paul galloped up on his horse. He stared at them anxiously. "Are you guys okay? What happened here? Where's Quicksilver?"

"She has headed back to the barn, I believe." Carlos's voice was cold with fury. "What has happened is that whoever saddled that horse did not cinch it tightly. My friend could have been seriously wounded when her saddle slid around the horse. When you are dealing with inexperienced riders, there is no excuse for such carelessness. I presume you will look into the matter and the culprit will be fired."

"What? No—" Lily looked up with fresh alarm. "I don't want—"

"Hush, Lily." He turned his attention back to Paul. "We will return to the barn, but I will talk to you about this when you get back with the others."

Paul glanced nervously toward the other riders and then back at Carlos. He nodded and cantered away.

"Now, Lily. Are you hurt anywhere?" Carlos tilted her chin up so he could look into her eyes. They were still black with fear. He lightly stroked her hair.

"I don't think so. I was just very scared. I thought I was going to—" She shuddered. "Thank you. You saved my life." Lily gazed at him in awe.

"I always did want to be a hero," he joked uncomfortably. "Do you feel safe enough if we ride back slowly together?"

She paused and then whispered, "I feel safe with you."

"All right. Then let's get you on this horse properly. Swing that leg over the horse's neck." He lifted her into the saddle in front of him. He looped his arms around her waist and leaned forward to kiss the top of her head. "I am very relieved that you were not hurt. I was extremely scared, too."

They rode slowly to the barn in silence. Carlos was holding her perhaps a little closer than was necessary, but he couldn't seem to relinquish his grip. When they neared the barn, she turned to look at him.

"Were you telling the truth that it wasn't my fault? You weren't saying that to make me feel better?"

"*Dios, no*, Lily. The saddle should not move, no matter what you do on the horse."

"You know," she added sadly, "in all those horse stories I read, riding sounded so much easier. I wish I hadn't tried it now."

"It *is* easy. We will go again." He continued, despite her sudden tension, "But next time, I will saddle your horse and we will go out, just the two of us."

"I don't think they let you go out alone."

"After today's fiasco, they will do anything we ask, for fear you might sue them."

"I wouldn't do that. It was an accident."

"Well some people might. Besides they will do whatever I request."

"Yeah, I guess there are people like that."

Carlos dismounted quickly and then helped her down. One of the barn hands came out to take the bay.

"Did Quicksilver come back?" Lily asked.

"Yeah. That mare has a bad habit of holding her breath when you're tacking her. I'm glad you're okay. I'll speak to Paul about it," the employee said.

"He knows," Carlos said darkly and pulled Lily toward the hotel. Before they'd gone more than ten steps, he stopped suddenly. "You are limping. What is wrong?"

"I must've banged my leg. It's not bad." She started to walk again.

"This leg?" He kneeled in front of her, blocking her way. He tried to pull up her pant leg to see her injury but the narrow boot cut was too tight. His hand brushed the back of her calf and she flinched in pain. "Sorry." With a muttered curse, he scooped her up to carry her the rest of the way to the hotel.

"This is embarrassing, Carlos. I can walk for heaven's sake. Please put me down."

"Pretend it is a romantic gesture, if it will make it less embarrassing," he told her with a smile. "I want to be sure you haven't broken anything. If you are in shock, you may not feel it yet, but you could do more damage."

*

Lily's face flushed at his suggestion. If he only knew how hard she was trying to rein in her attraction to him. Maybe it was the extra adrenaline from being so frightened, but she had been so sexually aroused by him riding back to the barn, she'd worried he would sense it. And now as he held her, she couldn't help but react to his muscular arms. And he smelled so good, like sandalwood and vanilla.

She gave in and put her arms around his neck. She felt his shoulder muscles relax. But when she rested her head on his shoulder, he tensed again. *Was he regretting his offhand comment about it being a romantic gesture?* She tried to think of something to say and then she felt a light pressure against the top of her head. *He kissed me. Or was he just shifting and his chin bumped my head?*

Lily gave up trying to figure out what was going on. When they reached her room, they would look at her leg, see that it was fine, and then maybe discuss plans for dinner. At least she'd shaved her legs this morning. When they arrived, she took the key card from around her neck and pressed it to the lock. Carlos opened the door and carried her in.

"Okay, now you can put me down." She smiled at him. He set her down very carefully, all the time gauging the expression on her face.

"I want to see that leg to be sure you are all right," he told her sternly.

Lily grabbed some shorts from the dresser and walked slowly into the bathroom, her lips pressed firmly together as she fought the urge to limp. She took off her jeans and was shocked to see a clear impression of a horse's hoof imprinted on her calf. *Well, that explains the pain.* She felt carefully for any tears or breaks around the mark.

"Lily? Are you all right?" Carlos called from outside the bathroom, sounding impatient.

"Yup. It's just a bruise." She came out in her shorts and showed him. "I checked and there's no ligament or bone damage."

His lips tightened into a thin line. "That looks painful. I will get a doctor."

"No, thank you. It'll be fine," she reassured him.

"I will get you some ice."

"No." She hugged him impulsively. "But thank you for everything."

His arms tightened around her and he rested his chin on her head. He didn't seem to want to let her go. And, she realized suddenly, she didn't want him to either.

Lily turned her head and kissed the hollow above his collarbone. His body tensed in response and she paused to assess his reaction. He didn't pull away, so she quietly kissed her way up his neck. A low groan in his throat vibrated against her lips. He pulled her face up to meet his and kissed her hungrily. His hands held her hard against his body, his erection evident through the layers of clothes. Her body responded instantly to his need.

She fumbled with the buttons on his shirt, desperate to feel his skin beneath her fingers. The last button released and she ran her hands up his chest, pushing his shirt off his shoulders. He let go of her briefly, allowing his shirt to drop to the floor. Her hands traversed up his hard abdomen and through his chest hairs. His muscles twitched as her fingertips circled his nipples.

She paused to raise her hands above her head while Carlos removed her t-shirt, then again, when he lowered his head to kiss her breast through the thin fabric of her bra. She barely noticed when her bra joined the growing pile of clothes on the floor. All she felt was the pounding need within her as he licked and sucked at her aching breast. Her fingers played with his hair while she urged him to the other breast.

With minimum effort, Carlos backed her toward the large bed. He slid her shorts and underwear down her legs in one easy movement and Lily found herself standing naked in front of him. Suddenly, she panicked. She wanted to cover up, or run, but neither seemed to be an option. She froze as she tried to figure out what to do.

His hand paused on her breast and Lily took in a shaky breath. He must have sensed her discomfort. But did she want him to stop? Here was an opportunity to have sex that probably wouldn't be painful. She unclenched her jaw, relaxed her fingers, and stretched up to kiss him.

He responded immediately, reclaiming her mouth. His thumb circled her breast, teasing the sensitive nipple making her want more as she arched against him. He trailed his mouth along her jaw line until he was nibbling on her earlobe.

"Mmm, yes," she murmured.

He pushed her back onto the bed and moved his hand up between her legs, his lips again feasting on her breast. Lily tensed instinctively against his probing fingers and forced herself to relax again. He was gentle as he coaxed her thighs open. He kissed down her stomach. She jerked up when his tongue took over where his fingers had been. She started to protest but when he pulled gently at her with his mouth her body rhythmically drew him in.

He slipped his finger inside her and her body pulsed around him. She tensed unable to breathe. *What the—it was like an electrical storm raged deep inside her and she wanted—no needed—* She heard the low moaning before realizing it was coming from her own mouth. Her fists gripped the bedding. Her stomach muscles contracted and she crunched forward, jamming her hand over her mouth to stifle a scream. Then wave after wave of tremors flew though her body releasing all the tension. *Holy crap.* He kissed her stomach and she shuddered, her body still not her own.

"*Bella.* What is wrong?"

Lily wiped away the tears streaming down her face as she regained her breath. It wasn't something she could explain. She wasn't even sure what she'd just experienced.

He gathered her into his arms and rolled onto his back. "Did I hurt you?" He sounded confused.

"No." Lily tried to stifle her sniffles. "I'm sorry."

"For what?"

"Nothing. Please just hold me." God, he must think she's a basket case.

"Lily. I'm sorry. It has been a scary day for you." He stroked her back.

She snuggled into his embrace relieved he'd found a reason for her inappropriate reaction. She definitely didn't want to relate the pain and humiliation she'd previously experienced with sex. Carlos's lovemaking had been a revelation to her. She feathered her hand across his chest. He gazed down at her warily as her hand ventured lower.

"Only if you mean it," he cautioned.

"Oh, but I thought—"

"You don't have to. But I only have so much control here."

Oh damn. She hadn't even thought about protection. Would he demand she go down on him? "Do you have a condom?"

"Yes."

"Good." She raised herself up on one elbow and leaned over to kiss him tentatively licking around his lips until he captured her tongue. His torso was amazing; soft skin covering hard muscles responding to her every touch. She undid the top button of his jeans, both excited and nervous to see how much the straining jeans concealed.

With a smile, he took a condom out of his pocket then removed the rest of his clothes. She tried not to stare at the huge penis suddenly pointing toward her. Just because it's big doesn't mean it will hurt.

He slid back on the bed beside her and pushed her against the pillow.

"Tell me what you want, *bella*."

"You." She smiled at him hoping she looked confident and brushed his hair back from his face.

Carlos caught her hand and kissed her palm. Then he slowly worked his way up the inside of her arm tantalizing her with soft kisses and little bites. She trembled, her skin quivering with his touch. He shifted from her shoulder down to her breast, playing her body like a musician, each touch striking a different note.

He sheathed himself before easing inside her. She tensed at the thickness stretching her. Damn, this part was going to be painful. Then Carlos stopped. Lily searched his face to see if he was annoyed with her.

"You are so warm and tight." He smiled as he lowered his face to hers and kissed her. His tongue explored her mouth, pulsing with a sensuous rhythm. She gasped as his fingers stroked between her legs enticing her to open wider. She circled her legs around his thighs and pulled him in to his full length. She wanted to sustain the glorious feeling as he withdrew and then pumped within her. Grabbing his butt she tilted her hips up to meet his thrust.

"Yes. More. Harder." Her muscles contracted as she clung to him wringing out the last of her release. His guttural cry as he ground into her made her feel oddly proud.

She stared at his perfect features glistening with a faint sheen, not wanting to him to withdraw. It felt like something amazing had passed between them. Then again, what did she know? She'd only been with a man who'd used sex as a weapon. This must be what normal people did. She needed to keep it in perspective. She was too intelligent to mistake making love for anything deeper.

He rolled off of her, kissed her forehead, and walked to the bathroom. She crawled under the sheet and wondered what to do. Would he think it strange that she was still lying there, when he came out of the bathroom? Or was that the common practice when you have sex in the early afternoon? She was still pondering when he returned.

*

Carlos smiled at her face peeking sweetly out from under the sheet. She looked so fresh and innocent. As he got closer, he saw that the sun had added a few faint freckles across the bridge of her nose.

"Room for one more person under there?" he asked and she silently lifted the edge of the sheet for him. After he climbed in, he pulled her over so she was resting in his arms with her head on his shoulder. "You are very beautiful."

"You too." Lily answered, and then she blushed.

"Thank you." Carlos played with a lock of her hair. The silence between them that followed felt comfortable, but there was so much he wanted to know about this woman, he didn't know where to start. "So what type of art do you do?"

"Sculpture. I studied drawing and painting as well. But mostly I sculpt."

"With clay?"

"Well, actually, whatever I can get my hands on." She laughed. "A friend at The Art Students League got us a good deal on some marble last year, so I did a few pieces in that." Carlos nodded encouragingly and she continued, "And now the school has a new welding department and I'm finding that I really like working in metals."

"Are these abstracts, then?"

"It depends. The medium sorta defines the style. What I mean is I have a firm idea of how I want something to go. And if I'm working in clay, then I can usually produce what is in my head. But with stone, you can't go against your material. Sometimes you can persuade, but other times you have to let the stone guide you. Metal is somewhere in between. You can bend it to your will to a degree, but you have to be decisive. If you change too often you'll weaken its structure." She paused and shook her head. "I'm sorry. I'm rambling on and boring you."

"I love to hear you speak of art. You have passion. I wish I could see your work."

"No. I'd be too embarrassed to show you. So how come you go to the same vacation spot each year?"

"I don't…oh, because I have been here before. Actually I am here on business."

"What kind of business do people do at expensive resorts?"

Carlos kissed her forehead as he considered his response. "My company has purchased a cruise line and I am here to see about buying this resort for a destination."

"Wow. So you're like a purchasing agent for your company. That must be an amazing job."

Should he correct her? No. It would be better if she didn't know that he owned the company. "I enjoy my work," he answered evasively.

"I can't imagine why. But maybe you should stretch it out a bit and get them to send you to a few other great resorts, as well." She wrinkled her nose in distaste. "I guess that'd be dishonest. But what if they want to buy a bunch of restaurants and sent you everywhere to eat? Man, I'd love to be a buyer. I never knew that was a career option."

Carlos couldn't help laughing at her enthusiasm. "Well, you could also be a restaurant critic or a travel writer. They get paid to eat or travel."

"That's true. Where did I go wrong?" She ran her fingertips across his chest. "I love how your chest hairs feel so sproingy."

"Then do I get to play with the hairs on your chest?"

"I don't have a hairy chest," she shot back.

"Let me see." He ducked under the sheet to check. "I'm just going to make sure they aren't hidden," he called out as he began to suck on one nipple. "I'm going to check the other one. A man must be thorough." He heard her delightful giggle as he tickled her ribs.

Carlos was surprised at how much fun it was to play with Lily. The women he usually bedded weren't the kind you could tease. In comparison, they seemed very jaded. And to be honest, he'd never seen himself as a playful person either. It was too bad that he only had her for a week. He banished the thought from his head as a new realization came to him.

"We should go get some lunch." He poked his head out from under the sheet.

"Really?" She laughed. "I hadn't thought that was what was on your mind."

"Well I was thinking of other entertainment, but I don't have another condom," he admitted. "It is afternoon, so food is not a bad idea. Just not my first choice."

"I need a shower before I go out in public."

"Of course. We could try out the Jacuzzi together." He gave her a hopeful look.

"I'd rather have a shower at the moment. It's too warm for a Jacuzzi."

"Very well then, come along." He pulled the sheet away and held out his hand to her. Something odd flickered in her eyes, almost like she was embarrassed for him to see her naked. He must be mistaken. Artists were not prudes.

"You want to shower together?" she asked uncertainly.

"Of course." His eyes caressed her body. She was delectable, but seemed unaware of the power of her sexuality. "I will make sure you clean those hard to reach places. Hurry, we don't have all day."

"Yes we do," she corrected him. "We're on vacation."

He pulled her out of bed, stopping just short of the bathroom to kiss her on the nose. Then he lowered his mouth to her lips and taunted her with a slow tantalizing kiss. She melted against him and it occurred to him again that she might be very difficult to leave when the week was over.

Chapter Three

Lily ate one last bite of chicken and reluctantly pushed her plate away. It seemed criminal to leave so much food, but the waiter had given her enough lunch to feed two people. Forget about sending the leftovers to China—she just wished she could give it to the blind homeless man on Fifty-seventh Street in Manhattan. There probably were hungry people here in the Dominican Republic, too. But she couldn't redirect the food, so there was no point obsessing about it. In less than a week, she'd be back home, counting quarters to buy her morning bagel and coffee on the way to school. She should enjoy the decadence while she could.

"You are finished?" Carlos was peering at her strangely. Had she been making faces worrying about the leftovers? He'd think she was nuts.

"Yes. It was great, but they give you such huge helpings." She looked at his unfinished plate and then at the few other stragglers in the restaurant. "Do you think anyone eats this much?"

"Some, but I think mostly the resort over serves to make you feel you are getting more for your money."

"But it's a waste. They should offer smaller portions with second helpings available."

"True. I will pass that along if we buy the resort."

"You're making fun of me," Lily complained.

"A little. Few people complain about getting too much for their money." He smiled and added, "But you are right, it is wasteful." He looked at his watch. "I'm sorry. I must take a conference call, but we will meet for dinner. Let's say, I'll be at your door at seven. It will be formal attire." Carlos kissed her lightly on the cheek and strode off.

Lily watched him go with a slight feeling of bewilderment. He hadn't even given her an option on dinner. Not that she didn't want to go with him, but she wasn't used to someone else making plans for her. Then again, now that she was suddenly alone, she felt unsure about what to do next. She glanced at her watch. She still had time to check out the games and fitness rooms and get in a long swim.

She finished her juice and stood to leave. A spasm of pain shot up her leg. She'd forgotten about that. First things first, she scooped up two glasses of ice from underneath the ever-present display of fresh fruit and walked to the concierge to ask for a plastic bag. The lady at the desk was surprised by her request but managed to find one.

Lily headed out to a lounge chair beside the pool and rested her bruise on the makeshift icepack. That at least should reduce the swelling. She should've iced it right away, but she hadn't wanted to do it in front of Carlos. Odd that. Instead she'd let him make love to her. Actually, she'd made the first move on him.

Was she seriously crazy? There was no way they could have a real relationship. They lived in different countries and had nothing in common. He was so sophisticated and probably quite wealthy. Plus he was gorgeous and self-assured. It was obvious he was only playing with her until his real girlfriend turned up. And how was she going to deal with that?

She didn't want to admit it, but she was falling for the guy. Who wouldn't? He had the charm and good looks of a movie star. And the way he looked at her and touched her, made her feel like the most desirable woman in the world. *Hah! He was a good actor.* Danny had hated her figure; her boobs were too small and her legs were too pale and muscular. And last time she looked she was still the same. But even if Carlos was just pretending to like her, she still couldn't bear the heartache of watching him disappear. Well, it was too late to worry about that now. Getting hurt was a done deal.

*

Lily was surprised at how quickly the rest of the afternoon passed. She'd wondered if lacking Carlos's company would leave her feeling stranded or lonely. Instead she enjoyed exploring, trying to remember everything to share with him later. And she spent a fair bit of time trying to decide what to wear to dinner. She never was sure what people meant when they said formal.

Aunt Lilith had given her a slinky black dress that she said one of her tai chi buddies had passed along. Considering it was exactly her size and looked brand new, Lily suspected her aunt had bought the dress and lied so Lily wouldn't feel guilty. The dress fit, but it wasn't her style. She felt overexposed with the low cleavage and the fabric's clinginess. But her one other dress was cotton and perhaps erred on the casual side.

In the end, she chose the black one because then she could wear dark nylons to conceal her burgeoning bruise. And, she admitted, she also wanted to show Carlos that she could be sexy. Not that she could compete in any way with the gorgeous, Spanish beauties he was probably used to dating, but at least she could try to look good.

Lily was especially careful with her make-up, going for the smoky eyes and dramatic lips they were showing in all the fashion magazines. It looked so easy, but trying to get it right took ages. After she'd finished she had to keep resisting the urge to wash it all off again. It just looked weird on her. She let her hair dry into its naturally wavy state. At seven o'clock, she was ready and perched anxiously on the edge of her bedside desk rereading the resort brochures. A firm knock rattled her door. She jumped in response and then gasped as her bruised calf reacted to her sudden movement. With a deep breath, she practiced her limp-free walk to the door.

"Are you ready to—?" Carlos stopped mid question when he saw her. Lily shrank back in embarrassment as his eyes swept eagerly over her.

"*Dios*, Lily. You are absolutely stunning."

He stepped into her room and pulled her into his embrace. One hand held her firmly against his hard body while the other slid through her curls. Lily could hardly breathe as he kissed his way down from her temple to her ear, murmuring soft endearments in Spanish. Then his lips finally made their way to her own.

She was barely aware of anything other than the raw need he evoked in her. Her fingers clutched at his muscular back, helping to fuse his body to hers. His hand climbed up her waist and she turned slightly with a moan as he cupped her breast. Lily's entire body was on fire and she cried out when Carlos suddenly backed away. He looked a little sheepish as he rearranged her dress back into place.

"You make me forget myself. But if we do not stop now, we will not make our dinner reservation." His dark eyes still caressed her body longingly.

Lily had to clear her throat before she could speak.

"We could go there another night," she suggested.

"Alas, the taxi awaits us."

"This restaurant isn't in the resort?" Lily felt a surge of panic that she quickly squelched.

"No." His playful grin lessened her worries. "It is much better. You'll see."

She ran her hand up the front of his burgundy silk shirt. He looked so debonair in his perfectly tailored suit that she wanted to remove it immediately. She was shocked by her own lust. Her touch seemed to inflame him and she was soon pinned against the door in a passionate kiss. He paused and cleared his throat. "We must go."

She trotted carefully to the bathroom to repair her lipstick.

"Okay, I'm ready," she nodded when she returned. "But this had better be exceptional food." She lightly hip-checked him and sauntered out the door.

*

They took a taxi drive along a scenic winding road that overlooked the dazzling blue ocean dancing in the light breeze. Lily was almost disappointed when they reached their destination until she saw the beautiful pink building with a terrace surrounded by a massive garden exploding with flowers. The intoxicating scent of a thousand blooms lightly tickled her nose. And the colors were so vibrant she could barely believe they were real. Maybe she could come back later to sketch them.

"This place is incredible."

"Wait until you taste the food." Carlos steered her through the ornate wooden doors and instantly her mouth watered from the luscious aromas wafting through the restaurant.

A handsome man in a black suit hurried toward them and enveloped Carlos in a bear hug with kisses to both cheeks. "*Hola, Carlos. ¿Como estas, mi amigo?*" Then he looked at Lily and exclaimed, "So this is the reason you take so long to visit me. I wonder when my best friend comes to town and does not visit for two days. Carlos, you will introduce me to this beautiful woman."

"I think not, Tony. I cannot trust you." Carlos strategically moved between her and his friend. "Lily, you must not believe anything this man tells you. He is a marvelous chef, but I will not speak for his character."

"Lily, is it?" Tony stepped around Carlos and took her hand, bowing low over it. "Tony Consuelo. You must allow me to save you from this evil man. But first, we will feed you." He led them to their table with a flourish. "I had to oust four members of the Estonian royal family from your table, but for you Carlos…"

"You are too good, Tony. But I believe Estonia does not have a royal family."

"*¡Basta!* No wonder their crowns looked plastic." He pulled out a chair for Lily. "Have a seat. Raul will be here with your wine in a moment."

"*Gracias*, Tony. Could we also get some Perrier for Lily?" Carlos requested.

"*Claro.*" Tony turned away.

When they were alone again Carlos said, "Now if you will permit me to order for you, I make only one small request. You must save enough space for dessert. Tony has created a chocolate decadence that is famous around the world."

"Well then, why don't we start with dessert and see if we have room left over for the first course?"

"It is a good idea," Carlos concurred, "but no."

"So how do you know Tony?"

"We went to school together and were both on the university football team. He was an amazing striker until he got fat." He threw the last comment over his shoulder as Tony walked by, and received a cuff on the head in return.

"Is that the guy who throws the ball?" she asked and then blushed at his amused expression. She should've just smiled and nodded. It was embarrassing how little she knew about sports.

"No, not American football. This was real football, where you kick the ball with your feet."

"Oh, you mean soccer, like Beckham plays."

"*Ah si. Exactamente.*" Carlos turned his attention to Raul, who had brought their beverages. The two men conversed in rapid and animated Spanish then Raul bowed and quickly departed.

"So did you study at university to be a buyer, or did you work your way up into that position?"

"I have a business degree."

"But is that what you always wanted to do?" she persisted.

"No. What I wanted to do was to become an American cowboy." He smiled when Lily laughed. "I am serious. I grew up on a farm outside of Barcelona and we had several horses. I was a big fan of the Italian westerns as a child and really wanted to be a cowboy. I practiced all sorts of daredevil riding and planned to move to America. My family was supportive, to a point, but my father was determined that I go to university. After all, I was the only son. When my father died, I went into business. The rest is history. And you? Did you always want to be a sculptor?"

"Not really." She furrowed her brow. "I knew I didn't want the professions that they were promoting at school, but I didn't have a clue about what I did want. High school art class was the first thing I felt I excelled at, but I didn't think I could make a living at it. Then I moved to New York to live with my aunt. She helped me get into art school. And the rest, as you say, is history."

"Do you have any brothers or sisters?"

"No, it was just me and my mom." Lily ducked her head and took a sip of her water.

"I am sorry. It must have been terrible when you lost your mother. I hadn't realized that you had no other family."

"I have my aunt." She quickly changed the subject. "So how long are you in the Dominican Republic?"

"Just for a week. This is enough time for me to turn you into a professional horsewoman." Carlos reached over and held her hand. "It is important to me. I know if given proper instruction, you will love riding as much as I do. I have spoken with the stable; they will let us have two horses tomorrow at ten. I will personally saddle your horse and we will go as slowly as necessary until you feel comfortable. Will you trust me?"

"Okay. But I don't know if—"

"It will be fun and you will be marvelous." Carlos turned as Raul brought two bowls of seafood chowder. "*Gracias.*" He winked at her and said with a smile, "I informed Raul that you wanted less of the main course, so you wouldn't have to worry about not finishing your meal. But if you want more of anything, tell me."

"Thank you." She tasted the soup. "Mmm, this is fantastic. Is this a Spanish soup?"

"No. The menu here is mostly French cuisine. Tony tells me

it is what the tourists want, although he occasionally adds in specialties from home."

As soon as they'd finished their soups, Raul brought out the main course. Lily was almost sorry to see that the portions were small, as the food was amazing. Carlos's plate was not noticeably larger than hers, so she decided he'd been pulling her leg. It was again some type of seafood, but this time presented in a light sauce over delicately seasoned rice. Even the vegetables had an extra fresh flavor to them.

"This is bad," she informed Carlos sadly. "I'll never be happy with normal food again after this vacation."

"I am sorry. I will have Tony send you care packages in New York. Would you like some coffee with your dessert?"

"Yes, please." She was looking forward to chocolate, of course, but even more so she was fantasizing about their after dinner plans. She blushed as she noticed Carlos staring at her. Is this how vacation romances went? You have as much sex as you can, in a short period of time, and then go your separate ways. The trouble was that for her it was much more than just sex. She was fascinated by him as a person. He was self-assured and dignified, but he was also fun.

Her colleagues at The Art Students League seemed to be either "serious artists" with no sense of humor or young kids fresh out of high school playing at being artists. She had never fit in with either type. But Carlos made her feel acceptable, not like she was an outsider peering through a window.

Maybe that was what these affairs were for—well aside from the amazing sex—so that strangers could meet you with no preconceptions and, since it wasn't long term, they weren't looking for your faults. Of course, Carlos didn't have any faults, except perhaps that he was too perfect.

"What is it, Lily? You look so serious."

She gave her head a shake. "Nothing. I just remembered that I have to mail my aunt's postcard tomorrow, so it arrives before

I've been back too long." She winced at how lame her answer had been.

Luckily, Raul arrived with a dessert for Lily and coffees for them both.

"You don't eat dessert?" She feigned shock. "In New York you'd be hanged for a witch for that kind of behavior."

"I will have to remember that." He chuckled.

The dessert was incredible. It was a layered concoction with chocolate crunchy cake on the bottom, covered with chocolate fudge, then a thin layer of something white and gooey, and drizzled with a chocolate sauce. The cake had a frill of whipped cream, looping decoratively down the sides. Lily resisted the urge to lick her plate clean.

"Okay, that was the most amazing dessert ever," she told Tony when he joined them.

"It is my secret weapon to deliver world peace. We will get all the leaders in one room and serve my Chocolate Amore. No one can be killing when they are enjoying chocolate," he declared.

"I think it'd work," Lily agreed.

"Should I tell you some dark secrets about Carlos?" Tony asked with a playful grin.

"Oh yes."

Carlos stood abruptly. "I think we should be going now, before there is one less restaurateur in the Dominican Republic."

"Ah, he is worried I will tell you about his Achilles heel. Ask him about his rescue program for horses. People, he can leave bleeding on the street, but a wounded horse from a bullfight and Carlos is charging in there with bandages."

"A little simplified," Carlos complained. "Meanwhile, we really should be on our way. Will you call us a car, Tony?"

"Yes, of course. And Lily, when you get tired of this ne'er-do-well, let me know. I will show you how a *real* Spaniard treats a beautiful woman." He bowed low with an exaggerated kiss to her palm.

She giggled as Carlos pulled her determinedly toward the door.

"Your friend is very nice," she told him once they were outside. "Of course, I'd say that of anyone who fed me that well."

"I'll try to remember that."

He put his arm around her in the car and they rode back to the resort in companionable silence. Incredible that she could feel so happy with Carlos, knowing that she only had five more days with him. But she wasn't going to ruin their time together, moping about how rotten she would feel afterward. She snuggled into his embrace and was rewarded with a soft kiss against her hair.

"Did you want to go dancing, to the casino, or…?" Carlos asked as he helped her out of the car.

"Not really, unless you'd like to," she answered uncertainly. She'd assumed they would rush back to her room.

"Good."

His arm tightened around her waist and he steered her toward the elevators. She glanced at him in surprise when he pushed the button for the fourth floor.

"My place, this time." He smiled. "I don't want you to get bored."

When he unlocked his door the first thing she saw was a massive dark wood table surrounded by high-backed leather office chairs. An easel with a flipboard, pull-down screen and closed cupboards completed the office aura. She stopped, confused.

"Come." He held out his hand to her and pulled her through to the inner room. There, the suite resembled hers although he had windows on two sides of his room, one showing a similar beach view as hers, and the other revealing the trees and flowers to the west. Aside from a small notebook and pen resting by the bed, there was no personal items lying about whatsoever. Lily tried to think what he'd seen in her place; hairbrush, shoes on the floor, her book, sketchpad, pens and pencils, and she'd been trying to be neat.

A soft kiss to the back of her neck interrupted her thoughts. She turned to him and was immediately locked in his embrace. In a matter of seconds her black dress fell to the floor. Her stockings and heels landed in a pile a little closer to the bed. Soon she was naked and falling backwards onto the bed with Carlos pinning her down.

"I have been dreaming of this all day," he murmured huskily in her ear. "I could not do anything when I thought about this place on your neck." He nibbled lightly, sending shockwaves shooting through her system.

"Let me—" she tried to get his shirt undone but was distracted by his roving hands. "Please, I want—"

"No," he growled. "I have been waiting too long."

She moaned as his hands seemed to be everywhere on her, stroking and molding her body into a liquid state of arousal. Her hips shifted to encourage his skillful plundering. It was happening too fast and yet she wanted it faster. She bit her hand to muffle her screams as her body convulsed in desire. The shuddering slowly abated and he rolled over and wrapped her in his arms. She rested her head on his shoulder while she caught her breath. Then she finally undid the last few buttons on his shirt. She felt his chuckle in his chest.

"You really don't like being the only one naked."

"No, it's not that…" she protested weakly.

She felt strangely relieved when he didn't pursue the topic and instead removed the rest of his clothes. Lily couldn't help staring at his body. The broad, muscular shoulders, his tanned chest with the smattering of curly hair, and his amazing abdomen, lean but muscled, drawing her eyes down further. She blushed when she realized that she was practically drooling.

She had seen many naked men in the course of her art studies, but he was more than a figure to be learned and replicated. Also the models had never been in a full state of arousal. Unconsciously she licked her lips as he lowered himself back onto the bed.

*

Carlos almost lost control when he saw the raw desire on Lily's face. It made him want to dive deep inside her until she begged for mercy. Instead, he found a condom, sheathed himself, and slid onto the bed beside her. He kissed her lips gently and began exploring her body again. He sensed her impatience as her leg curled around his waist and pulled him over her.

She reached up, bit his neck, then whispered urgently in his ear, "I need you inside me, now."

Carlos rushed to do her bidding. Her warmth enveloped and pulled him into her depth. He groaned with pleasure at the sensation of her stretching around him. It felt so good to slowly glide through her moist heat. He trailed his hand down her upper thigh and pushed her leg up toward the ceiling. Lily gasped in surprise and then moaned as he pushed himself even further inside.

Her breath quickened and her fingers dug into his back, urging him on. He loved the way her quiet voice pleaded with him and her hips rolled up to meet his. He slid his fingers between her legs. The result was an explosive reaction that took them both by surprise. Lily curled up and muffled her loud scream of pleasure against his neck. Her convulsions made his own release almost violent and he ground into her with a primal need. He clutched her tightly to him, driving his last thrust into her.

"*Dios*, Lily!" he exclaimed, burrowing his face into her neck.

There was something wild and real in the way she gave herself so completely. Suddenly he raised himself off her, fearing that he might be crushing her. His arms circled her and he looked down at her flushed face. He stroked her hair, feeling a strange need to protect her. From what, he had no idea.

He couldn't remember ever feeling so drained after sex. His legs were weak on the short walk to the washroom. But he was sated also. It felt like they had a deeper connection than just the physical act. He shook his head at his crazy thoughts as he crawled back into the bed. Was he getting old and soft? Yet there was something so different about the sexy yet timid way she melted into his embrace. During sex, she was so uninhibited, but now she seemed vulnerable. How could he unlock the mystery of this woman?

"Tell me something about your childhood, Lily," Carlos suggested as he shifted her comfortably onto his chest. She stiffened in his arms.

"Why do you always want to talk after sex?" She sounded disgruntled. "Aren't men supposed to just roll over and fall asleep? Am I doing something wrong?"

"*Dios, no.* But you are many contradictions. It makes me want to figure you out. Did your mother make hot dogs and apple pie for you when you were young?"

"Yes. It was a normal childhood." Her defensive answer piqued his curiosity more. "What about you? Did you have tacos and burritos for breakfast?"

"I told you about my childhood. You, *mi amor*, seem to be holding out. You know I will pull it out of you." He kissed her sweet smelling hair. "Tell me a secret."

He ran his hand down her spine, enjoying the smooth curve of her back. There was a long silence.

"My mother was an alcoholic." Her voice was strangely flat. "I never told anyone."

"Oh." He didn't know what else to say, so he continued to stroke her gently.

"I always told people she was sick, which was true. She'd be fine for a few weeks, just occasionally sloppy, and then she'd go on a bender where she'd be out of control for several days. When she was out of it, I learned to cook pancakes and mac and cheese, because that's what we had around the house. She was always sorry when she was sober, but she could never stay that way for long. We don't all lead 'happily ever after' TV lives in the States."

"I'm sorry, Lily."

"No. I don't want your pity. I'm not a victim. I was very lucky to have my aunt, who welcomed me with open arms. I was not an easy teenager."

"Well, you are a beautiful person now." He hugged her tight. "Thank you for telling me."

"I don't know why I did." She laughed sadly. "I never tell anyone. But it feels good to not lie about it, you know?" She curled up to his body and ran her hand just above his chest, lightly fanning the hair.

"Can I…" She paused. "Would you like me to give you a massage?"

"I would love that. But I might fall asleep," he warned her.

"That's okay. Lots of my clients do." She sat up beside him. "Roll over on your belly."

"You are very demanding when you work."

She put her palm on his back and then hesitated. "This feels weird massaging you without any clothes on."

"You mean me being naked, or you?" He chuckled.

"Both. I have sheets and towels for my clients' privacy." Lily's hand began slow circles around his shoulder blades.

"But you must have given your lovers massages before?"

Her voice was hesitant. "No." Her thumbs kneaded gently at first and then more firmly into his neck muscles. He was surprised, but happy with her answer.

He groaned when her fingers hit a particularly tight muscle.

She stopped. "Sorry, did that hurt?"

"Yes. But it was good pain." Carlos felt her work her way down his back, loosening muscles he didn't know he even possessed. She stopped and then straddled his legs, kneading the muscles leading into the small of his back. He must have drifted off to sleep when he suddenly felt her fingers spreading the bones in his foot. It was painful at first, then incredibly good as his foot stretched around her balled fist.

"Okay, turn over." She began to work on his other foot and then slowly moved back up his body. Her lips pursed with concentration as she worked her way up the front of his legs. She caught him watching her when she massaged his upper quads and her face flushed a pale pink.

"Close your eyes and relax," she whispered.

Carlos chuckled. Somehow, with a beautiful naked woman rubbing his thigh, relaxing wasn't at the top of his mind. Her eyes widened as his erection rose in front of her. He smiled, but closed his eyes as requested. It was thrilling to feel her hands manipulating his flesh just inches from where he craved her. Then he felt a warm, wet caress at the tip of his arousal. His eyes snapped open to see her slowly taking him into her mouth. The soft pull of her mouth retreated and then advanced again. The sensation was amazing. Reluctantly he pulled her up his body. Her eyes questioned him, and he struggled to find his voice.

"A condom…"

Lily smiled and took one from the bedside table. She ripped it open and rolled it over him with a deliberateness that drove him crazy. She licked her lips and then slowly lowered herself upon him. He thrust quickly into her but she pushed him down and lifted herself again with a maddening slow control. He cried out in frustration as she continued to taunt him. He reached for her breasts and cupped them in his hands.

With a low moan, she began to ride him harder. He grabbed her bottom and drove himself into her with abandon. He worried he would climax before her when she screamed out his name. All control lost, she pulled him hard inside her and her muscles clenched around him. His last seed emptied into her, Carlos pulled her into his embrace listening as her heartbeat raced against his. It was a few moments before he noticed the dampness on his chest. He raised her head and saw that she was crying.

"Lily?" He wiped the tears from her face with his thumb. She shook her head. He held her until he heard her breathing slow down and then he edged out from under her. After disposing of the condom, he climbed into bed beside her. He smiled as she sleepily spooned up against him.

Chapter Four

It was the most liberating feeling. She was cantering freely along the beach with the wind rushing through her hair and sand lightly flicking against her shins. Only the occasional spasm from her bruised calf reminded Lily of her previous terror. She laughed as Carlos flew by her on Midnight and waved his hand above his head like a crazy cowboy.

She hadn't thought she would ever feel safe on a horse, but he had slowly brought her around. This was his second day of riding lessons, and she was finally feeling comfortable. He was incredible with the animals. Even the stable hands seemed in awe of his abilities.

They slowed to a halt by a grassy area. The resort lay in the distance with the brightly clad tourists dotting the landscape. She was constantly captivated by the vibrancy of the colors inherent in both island nature and the visitors. Carlos reached over and squeezed her knee.

"You are amazing," he told her. "Practically professional."

His brown eyes looked at her with such pride that her eyes welled up with tears. She fought to regain control.

"Thank you. It's even better than I imagined when reading all those books."

"I'm glad you like it."

A pensive expression passed over his face. Was he thinking about the end of their vacation, too? In two days, they would fly off in opposite directions, probably never to see each other again. She certainly couldn't afford to visit him in Spain. And, although he was obviously better off financially, he had never suggested that he might fly to New York. So that left them soon parting for good. Lily tried to stop herself, but she kept mentally repeating the words "two days" like an ominous mantra.

They turned the horses back toward the resort. "Paul isn't going to be angry about us being out too long, is he?"

"No. He knows we will be back before three."

"You aren't making him feel guilty about my accident?" she asked cautiously.

"No. Have faith, Lily. He is being well paid for our time."

"Oh good. Hey, can I beat you at Ping-Pong when we get back?" Lily had taught him the game the day before and had finally found something she was better at.

"We will see." He rolled his eyes in mock despair. "I must spend a few hours on the computer before dinner."

"Don't worry. It won't take me long to wipe you out," she teased him.

"You can be a pain."

"I know. Oh, can we do karaoke tonight?"

"If you wish I will watch you sing. But I don't want to stay long."

"You have to sing, too, Carlos."

"*¡Dios, no!*" He looked appalled. "I do not sing."

"I bet you have a great voice," Lily insisted. "C'mon. It'll be fun."

"No. There is nothing you can say or do to make me sing. I would rather parade naked in front of a mongoose than to sing in front of anyone."

"Please."

"No. I am not kidding. Under no circumstances. If you tell me it is your birthday, I will hire someone else to sing 'Happy Birthday.' I cannot sing."

"You're a killjoy." Lily pouted, but she smiled when he used her ponytail to pull her in closer for a kiss.

*

Lily tried to keep her spirits up while she prepared for their dinner date. She had been fine during the Ping-Pong match, but as soon as she was apart from Carlos, the realization that they had so little time left together suffocated every other thought in her brain. He appeared unaffected by the fact that their affair would end soon. Was this what he did every vacation?

He'd said to dress up again for dinner, but she only had the red dress left, so that would have to do. At seven prompt, he was at her door. He seemed to like her dress, but wasn't rendered speechless. Nor did he carry her to the bed. Maybe he was already tiring of her.

"Ready to go, *mi ángelita?*"

"Yup."

Carlos put his arm around her waist, but otherwise seemed to ignore her during their walk to the restaurant. In fact, it wasn't until the hostess led them to their seats that he finally turned his brilliant smile to her.

"I am sorry, *bella.* I am a little distracted by the communications from Spain. I'm sure whatever the problem is my assistant will have fixed it by tomorrow, but the time delay in hearing from work makes me crazy." He rubbed his eyes and shook his head as if to clear his thoughts. "From now on, I am all yours this evening."

And true to his word, Carlos seemed attentive to her every desire. After dinner, he turned to her with a slow, seductive smile.

"What I want to do tonight is to take you dancing."

"Oh, I don't really dance," she stammered. Could she use her sore leg as an excuse? It really didn't hurt much anymore.

"You made me learn Ping Pong," he reminded her.

"But—"

"Please, *mi amor.*" He lowered his voice. "I will be your slave for the rest of the night."

"Does that mean you'll sing for me?"

"*¡Dios!* You are like a cur with a bone. No, anything but that."

"Okay, but you'll be sorry, slave." Lily pinched his butt and ran ahead in case he wanted to retaliate.

Entering the fancy ballroom, Lily was enthralled by the recessed rainbow lighting shining down on the raised band-stage. It was reminiscent of the elaborate dance halls in the old movies she used to watch on TV. The eight-piece band was dressed in white and black tuxedos, and they looked and sounded amazing as they played swing music. If only she were Kate Hepburn or Ginger Rogers in a beautiful flowing gown, then she would fit right in.

She was relieved when he led her to a table and she didn't have to embarrass herself right away. There were a few older couples on the floor, but the younger crowd was probably at the hip hop club or the disco. They sat for a few songs watching the stately couples gracefully dip and twirl. Then Carlos stood and held out his hand.

"Lily, may I have this dance?"

She didn't want to refuse, but she knew her limitations. "I'm really clumsy," she whispered in embarrassment. Her heart thudded in her chest.

"Come." He kept his hand out until she took it. "Just relax," he told her as he walked her to the dance floor. "It is my job to make you look graceful." He held her firmly away from his body and took a step forward.

She followed, but then looked down at his feet to see where he was going next. His finger under her chin tilted her face up to his.

"Look into my eyes. They will tell you which direction we will travel."

After a few moments, she began to anticipate his moves. He smiled at her growing confidence.

"You see? You are a natural dancer."

She stumbled on his foot as soon as he said it, but his firm grip held her steady.

She smiled sheepishly. "I think maybe I'm better at horseback riding, and that's not saying a lot."

"You need to be more confident and to trust me. Will you try another one?"

"Sure. It's kinda fun," she admitted. "But tell me if your feet get too sore."

"Never." He grinned. She loved how his eyes shone in the ballroom's sparkling lighting. He made her feel like she belonged in this fairy-tale setting.

*

Carlos relaxed his stance and drew Lily closer. She was so soft and pliant in his arms. He kissed her temple as they slowly circled the floor. She sighed, melting further into his embrace. The feel of her body fluidly moving against his was incredibly erotic. He had danced with many women more skilled and confident but had never felt such a raw connection on the dance floor. Her body was like an extension of his.

He lightly ran his fingertip beneath the back of her hairline and her skin shivered in response. It was thrilling how Lily reacted so vibrantly to his every touch.

Did they have to part? The question jumped into his head once again and this time with more persistence. He had known her for less than one week, but he still needed to know so much more about her. She fascinated him.

As a sculptor, she could live anywhere as long as she had the tools. He could certainly afford to set her up in a studio Barcelona. In fact, he was already a patron of many artists, just none that he was sleeping with. But it could get very messy when he tired of her.

Lily stumbled slightly and her thigh pressed firmly between his legs. The hard contact aroused him even more and he determined that somehow he would keep Lily in his life. The band finished the song, but he didn't want to release her. When he gazed down into her face, his passion was mirrored in her eyes. He kissed her and then murmured against her ear.

"May I escort you to your room?"

"Please." Her response was so breathy, he barely heard her, but there was no mistaking her desire. His hand remained on her back, keeping her pressed against him for a moment more. When he released her, it was like a physical loss.

They walked in silence back to her suite. Carlos resisted the impulse to draw her into a steamy kiss in the elevator, deterred only by the thought of the security camera. But as soon as they crossed her threshold, he turned to her with hunger. Then she was in his arms, kissing him back with a ferocity that surprised him. He quickly undid her dress and dropped it to the floor.

Carlos pulled her back against his body, massaging her flesh as she arched to encourage his roving hands. She released the button and zipper of his pants and he retrieved a condom from the pocket before his pants hit the floor. He bent over to suck greedily on her breast, her low moan sending him further over the edge. As his hand delved between her thighs, her moist heat pulled him in.

Swiftly sheathing himself in the condom, he picked Lily up and backed her against the door. Her expression was uncertain as she wrapped her legs around his waist, but when he lowered her onto him, her excitement built again. She shifted her hips and he filled her deeper. Carlos rhythmically thrust inside her. Then she whispered breathlessly in his ear, "Please…" and sank her teeth into his neck.

His body jolted in response and he drove himself into her. Lily muffled her scream into his shoulder and her body melted around his. She clenched him tighter, pulling him in, until his passion flowed into her. The last shudders left him depleted with his head resting against her forehead.

"*Mi amor*," he gasped, carrying her to the bed.

*

"That was—I've never—" Lily couldn't seem to finish her thoughts. Her mind reeled with the sensations careening through her body. Was it because they were parting that everything was so much more vivid? It felt like her muscles had liquefied and her bones were rubber as she lay there almost in shock.

Lily turned to look at Carlos. He was equally insensate. She drifted her palm over his abdomen, feeling his pulse still pounding. His arm slipped under her and drew her onto his chest. She felt rather than saw him smile as his lips pressed against her hair.

"Lily, what have you done to me?" he asked softly. He lifted her head to look into her eyes and ran the pad of his thumb across her lips.

"I don't know," she answered with a smile, "but I think I'm going to want to do it again."

Her tongue flicked out to taste his thumb. A soft chuckle rumbled in his chest. His eyes seemed to be searching hers, and she wondered what he saw there. She was trying so hard not to take their fling seriously. It wasn't his fault. He'd made no promises. She couldn't confuse her lust for something more. And with so little time left together, she should try to enjoy it to the fullest.

He furrowed his brows then let out a sigh as if deciding something.

"*Uno momento, mi amor.*" He kissed her and walked to the bathroom.

Lily lay on the bed trying desperately to think of something to entice Carlos with when he came out. Could she strike a provocative pose and have it not look silly? She tried a few and decided that she didn't have the confidence to pull it off. When he was staring at her with his lust-darkened eyes, then she felt sexy. But when she was alone, all the insecurities came rushing back in. She sat against the headboard and resolutely did not pull the blankets up to cover her nudity. As long as she wasn't pretending to be sexy, she was less self-conscious.

Carlos came out of the bathroom and stopped abruptly at the sight of her. His dark eyes raked her naked body with appreciation. A flush of sexual heat surged through her. Her eyes widened as she watched his body rise in response.

"Touch your breast," he commanded, in a low growl. Embarrassment flooded through her, but she slowly raised her hand to touch herself. She watched his reaction and it fascinated her. Her own mouth went dry with the thrill of watching him watching her. She moved her hand to her belly and then lower and his eyes almost burned her with their intensity.

"Oh yes," he murmured, stalking toward the bed. She couldn't tell how much of the heat infusing her body was from embarrassment or from lust, but she didn't care. All that mattered was the raw desire on his face. She spread herself open to him. Carlos quickly covered the space between them and joined her on the bed.

It was beautiful as they moved together in slow motion and with extreme gentleness to bring both of their bodies to the peak of arousal without allowing the release. The need became painful until she could stand it no longer.

"Now," she demanded as he continued to tempt her with feathery strokes.

"No." He paused to slowly and deliberately lick the center of her desire.

Her hips bucked in an effort to feel more, and he carefully pressed down on her belly. "Do you want this?" he taunted, sliding his long fingers within her. She gasped at the sensation building with each stroke.

Lily whimpered when his fingers retreated. She had never known such a combination of thrill and agony. Her neck was arched back in anticipation when she heard the now familiar sound of plastic being ripped.

"Oh please," she begged.

His weight settled between her thighs. Her relief knew no bounds, her response no inhibitions as he began to thrust inside her. She dug her fingers into his back and rose up to meet his every motion with a desperation that was foreign to her. He seemed to lose his own control and was now frantically driving into her, his hands spreading, pulling and molding her to his need. She couldn't control the scream wrenched from her throat. Carlos answered with a guttural cry of his own, pounding his final thrusts into her body. A fine sheen covered both of them as they collapsed together in a boneless mass.

Lily slowly drifted back to consciousness. Her mind struggled to deal with the moments before. She'd never felt such an out-of-body experience. It had been as though everything about her had disappeared except for the incendiary need. She was suddenly afraid to look at him. What if that had been nothing special for him?

*

Carlos peered down at Lily's face as he slowly withdrew. She looked sated and sleepy with her eyelids lowered as a calmness overcame the passionate woman who'd been writhing in his arms just moments before. She was so incredibly alive and attuned to his every touch, his every need. And he had intuitively known what she craved. Not in the controlled, calculating way that he knew the correct moves to thrill a lover, but in a primal way that his body seemed to call and answer to hers.

Carlos rested his head on her chest and listened to her racing heartbeat. He lightly stroked her taut abdomen. Her sensitive muscles quivered under his touch.

"*Mi amor*, you have put me under your spell," he whispered. "I will have to be very careful you do not get hanged as a witch in Spain."

Her body tensed at his remark, but she remained silent. That was probably lucky for him. It would be better if he worked out the details before he suggested she follow him home. His mind was working in several directions as he prepared for bed, but when he curled up against her, he relaxed, knowing that as long as he held her tight, everything would work out.

Chapter Five

Carlos grumbled quietly when his watch woke him at four-thirty in the morning. He didn't want to leave the comfortable warmth of Lily's body. His arm was draped over her and he shifted slightly to cup her breast, wondering if he had time for a little more play before he called his office. She sighed and snuggled back further into his embrace. He trailed his hand down her belly.

She seemed to be asleep, but her thighs opened for his exploration. He caressed lightly between her legs and felt her moisten and begin to pulse with his rhythm. He grabbed a condom and then eased himself between her legs. He wondered how sound a sleeper she really was, when her small hand reached around and pulled him in closer.

"*Buenos dias, mi amor*," he whispered into the back of her hair.

"Mmm," Lily agreed.

As he nuzzled the side of her neck, he heard her breath catch. His fingers awoke her slumbering senses even more until she cried out his name in a breathless plea. His own release was instantly triggered by hers. He dove into her, each shuddering thrust feeling like he was coming home.

After, Carlos held her firmly against him, wishing that time could stand still. With a sigh, he unwound her body from around his. If he completed his dealings quick enough, he could set in motion his plans for taking her home with him. That thought propelled him out of the bed and into his clothes.

Fully dressed he leaned over her recumbent body.

"I have to do some business, Lily, but I will see you after." He kissed her forehead and smiled at the blissful expression on her sleepy face. "*Mi angelita*," he whispered and quietly left the room.

*

In his suite an hour later, Carlos stared at his phone in total confusion. *It was impossible. Lily wouldn't do that.* Yet his assistant, Natalia, had no reason to lie about receiving the legal documents. Lilith Scott had filed suit claiming a broken wrist, whiplash, and trauma incurred when she fell in his gallery. Was Lily planning on getting a cast for her "injured" arm after her vacation?

¡Dios! How could he have been so blind to her true nature? But he had been fooled before. At least with Elena he had known of her mercenary nature. Lily had taken him in completely. She had feigned such shock when he had suggested suing the resort and stable, but of course, she had her eye on a much bigger prize. She was most likely waiting to see if she could catch herself a rich husband and if not, then she would file the lawsuit against the resort.

Carlos's blood ran cold when he realized how close he had come to making the biggest mistake of his life. Fortunately, he hadn't revealed his true worth, or she might already be claiming rape, paternity, or God knows what, against him.

His mind reeled as he paced his suite. He wanted to confront her, throw his knowledge in her face, and dare her to deny it. But it would be better for the lawsuit if she didn't know who he was. Natalia had been certain that Lily's suit had been only against his company, Stella Sociedad, and his people in New York.

A vision of Lily, with her head thrown back in wild abandon, rose unbidden into his mind. How could she have faked that? But if he accepted that she was a good enough actress to pull off the sweet, scrupulously honest, girl-next-door act, then he would have to believe that she also could pretend lust for him.

¡Dios! Her performance the first night he kissed her was worthy of an Oscar. She had seemed so young, so confused, and so innocent. And he had bought it all. *¡Stupido!*

The trouble was, as he recalled her magnificent performances in bed, he was getting aroused all over again. How could he want someone he knew was so deceptive? Normally he would be repulsed by such a creature. Well, he would have her one more time, and then let her know what he really thought of her. She would regret having toyed with him. Then when her lawsuit proceeded, he would again rake her over the coals. His body hummed in anticipation as he made his way back to her suite.

*

Her arms slicing cleanly through the warm water, Lily did a smooth crawl around the perimeter of the large, oddly shaped pool. She kept turning into little watery *cul de sacs* and getting disoriented. When she reached the end of the pool by the swim-up bar, she paused to count how many curves she had left to the stairs. It would've been easier to set herself the task of slaloming between the whirlpools. She set off again, this time doing the breaststroke for easier navigation. At least she had the pool to herself this early in the morning.

After Carlos left, she had been unable to go back to sleep. Her mind kept returning to the casual comment he'd made about her not being hanged as a witch in Spain. He probably didn't mean anything by it, but her heart kept latching on to the idea like a lifesaver. If she really pinched pennies and did a few extra massages per week, maybe she could afford a flight to visit him.

Lily was just getting back to her starting place when a familiar figure walked onto the terrace. His eyes homed in on her before he strode to the edge of the pool.

"Good morning. Did your business calls go well?" she asked with a smile.

Emerging from the pool, she wished she had a sexier bathing suit rather than this boring one-piece she'd bought for doing laps at the Y in New York.

"It was very informative." Carlos tossed her the towel she'd left on the chair. "I wondered where you were. I thought you preferred swimming in the ocean."

"I figured I should try the pool, just to say that I did." Lily wrung out her hair and then wrapped herself in the fluffy white towel. "Have you had breakfast yet?"

"I was hoping to find you still in bed," he said grabbing her arm and steering her away from the pool.

"Well, I couldn't sleep after you left." Lily struggled to keep up with his long strides. "Do you want to go back to my room?"

Something was odd about Carlos, but Lily couldn't quite put her finger on it. His smile seemed forced and his hand gripped her elbow a little too tightly. Her discomfort grew on the silent but swift journey back up to her suite.

Once inside, Carlos spun her to face him and ordered, "Take off your bathing suit."

Lily stared at him questioningly, but did as he asked. Strangely, she felt very exposed in front of him as his eyes almost dispassionately appraised her. She stepped forward to undo his shirt.

"No." Carlos brushed aside her hands and pushed her onto the bed. His voice softened slightly. "This is for me."

His gaze locked with hers while his hands began to slowly slide up her body. The concentration with which he circled slowly up her legs and to her inner thigh, unnerved her even as her internal muscles quaked in anticipation. He stroked her inner folds until her hips rose up to meet his fingers. Then he moved up her torso. His attention to her breasts was equally intense. He made her writhe in need, but he still seemed disconnected emotionally.

Again Lily tried to unbutton his shirt, but he pushed her hands away. Meanwhile his mouth feasted unabated on her breast. When she felt his teeth tease the tender skin between her neck and shoulder, she moaned and dug her hands into his hard muscular back, anticipating that he would next be kissing her lips. But suddenly he slid down her body. His tongue delved between her thighs. It seemed wrong, somehow too personal, given how distant he was acting.

"No." She tried to pull him up.

Carlos ignored her and his tongue began to tantalize her deep within. She moaned, as her body opened up for more. His fingers probed her inner depths until she cried out, lost in the whirling sensations he was creating within her. He continued until her body folded up in a tidal wave of convulsions. She collapsed in exhaustion, trying to drag much needed air into her lungs.

Her brain acknowledged the sound of his zipper, the rip of plastic, and then he was sliding inside her. She wanted to ask him to slow down, to let her recover, but he was driving into her with a need that her own body had to answer. His mouth was rough as he suckled one breast while his hand was tweaking and sweetly torturing the other. Lily's hips rose up to greet his with a strange sense of desperation. Then her legs were clenching his thighs, needing him to pour into her, to fill her completely. She called out his name and heard him groan in response. His body shuddered to its conclusion.

Lily shifted to gather Carlos in her embrace, but to her surprise, he withdrew and rolled away onto his side. She reached for him, but then drew back. His rigid back projected an icy aura.

"What is it?"

Carlos didn't answer but snatched his pants and padded off to the bathroom. Lily sat up on the bed with the sheet wrapped around her and stared at the bathroom door. When he emerged from the bathroom fully clothed, he still had that steely look in his eyes.

"Carlos, what's wrong?" She tried to keep her voice light.

"Why should anything be wrong? A little meaningless sex with a cheap *Americana* tart before I catch my flight home was just what I needed." His scornful smile made his words even harsher.

"What?" Lily gasped.

"Oh, I'm sorry. Maybe you thought you fooled me with your innocent act? Were you hoping I'd fall in love with you and make you my wife? *Bella*, girls like you are like leaves in a gutter. Don't flatter yourself that you bring anything new to the table. The 'massage' was good, but you should try plying your trade on older, more desperate men."

Lily watched Carlos stride out the door without a backward glance. She sat frozen for a few moments and then bolted for the bathroom. After retching into the toilet, she slumped against the side of the bathtub and tried to gather her scattered thoughts. Did he really think she was a prostitute? Had he assumed that from the start? What an awful thought.

She hadn't expected him to fall in love with her, but she thought he had at least liked her. How could he have pretended to care about her? Why did he bother teaching her to ride, feigned interest in her thoughts and life? How could she have been so totally blind to this cruel side of him?

Lily rose and stared blankly at her reflection in the mirror. She should be crying. She had just had the rug pulled out from underneath her. Her amazing vacation had turned into a shameful debauchery. She had fallen in love with a wonderful man who suddenly turned into a sadistic monster. And yet there were no tears streaming down her cheeks. She scrunched up her face to see if they were waiting to pour out. No. Only an ashen face with no expression stared back at her.

*

Filling out the customs form on the airplane, Lily realized that she hadn't brought any gifts back for Aunt Lilith. She hadn't even done any sketches she could offer. The first pinprick of tears began to form behind her eyes. Aunt Lilith had given her so much over the years, including this vacation, and she had spent the whole time thinking only of herself. Once the tears started, Lily couldn't stop them.

"I'm sure it will be okay, Miss." The large, sweaty, businessman sitting next to her reached out to pat her shoulder and then pulled back uncertainly. "Here you go." He handed her the paper napkin that had come with his drink.

"Thank you." She tried to discreetly blow her nose on the teeny napkin. "I'm fine, just…" She shook her head, embarrassed.

"Sure thing. If you need the flight attendant, you just push that little button there," he explained helpfully before turning back to his computer.

Lily picked the most depressing movie she could find on the movie channel in the hopes that she could divert her self-flagellation toward something else. Sure enough, between the bleakness of *Terms of Endearment*, and the distraction of airline food, she eventually got herself back under control. Somehow, she would find a way to make up for her thoughtlessness to Aunt Lilith during the next few weeks.

After only a couple of extra circles above JFK airport, the plane was permitted to land and begin the interminable taxi to the gate. As soon as the flight attendant requested the passengers remain seated, many got up and began rummaging in the overhead bins. Lily watched them in annoyance. Despite her lack of experience, even she knew that they wouldn't save any time by rushing now. There would be lines to get luggage, lines for customs, and probably lines just to get into the lines. She stared out the window at the gray New York weather. Was Carlos already home in sunny Barcelona? Was he thinking of her at all? No, she had been like the food, the horses, and the wine—an amenity to be enjoyed and then forgotten.

A bus to the train, to another train. As she exited the subway station on Greenpoint Avenue, Lily dropped the last of her change into the paper coffee cup on the ground. A sooty hand reached out from under the pile of gray blankets to claim her measly offerings. Barely registering the familiar landmarks, she dragged her suitcase the five blocks to her apartment. She parked her suitcase by the door and sank onto the couch that doubled as her bed. It had only been a week, but it felt like her whole life had changed. If only she hadn't gone to the barns on her first day and met Carlos. If only she'd turned down his invitation to dinner. If only she hadn't fallen in love with him.

Chapter Six

Deeper and deeper into her welcoming body, Carlos felt her hips rising up to meet his and he looked into her shining blue eyes.

"I love you, Carlos." It was a whisper, but he knew it was true.

"*Te quiero*, Lily," he gasped as he emptied himself into her. She would be his forever. His arms encircled her as he drifted off to sleep.

*

Carlos awoke several hours later feeling happy and refreshed. Then he remembered what Lily really was and the dark depression that had followed him home from the Dominican Republic once more fell upon him. His mood plummeted further when he walked into his office later that day.

"*¡Madre de Dios!* What is this?" Carlos pushed the buzzer on his phone to summon his assistant. His eyes were glued to Lily's face staring up at him from various tabloids on his otherwise pristine desk. The pain from realizing he'd been dreaming earlier bit into him once more. Why did Lily's deceit wound him so much deeper than Elena's? He'd known Lily for less time, but somehow she'd gotten right to his core.

"Welcome back, boss." Natalia placed another tabloid on top of the growing pile. She smiled cheekily. "I'd ask you how your business trip was, but…"

"No one was supposed to know where I went."

"We didn't tell anyone." She pointed to the picture of Lily lying on the chaise lounge. His stomach churned at the sight of her blue eyes glancing at him with feigned adoration. "Perhaps your mysterious friend did. *El Primo* is being very coy about her name to scoop the other tabloids."

"But she didn't know who I was." Carlos thought about it. Maybe the *Americana* had planned all along on trapping a rich foreigner and had the pictures taken on spec. She was certainly more cunning than he had taken her for. He should've been suspicious that first night. Lily Scott made his ex-fiancée look like a rank amateur when it came to sexual manipulation. He glanced at another headline and groaned.

"*¿DONDE ESTA ELENA, CARLOS?*" Good question. Where was Elena and what was she going to do now?

This was not going to be good for his image. And knowing Elena, she would use it for all it was worth. He'd assumed he would grant Elena a sum of money, not that she needed it, and she would disappear until her next high profile affair. But now with these photos, she'd claim public humiliation and require extra remuneration.

"Throw these out. I will deal with business first." He tore his eyes away from the photo of him kissing Lily while on horseback. He'd been so proud of her for riding again. Had it all been a set-up? How many people were involved? Carlos flipped through the documents Natalia placed before him.

"Where are the ones from the New York litigant?"

Natalia smiled. "That is my good news. I phoned Lilith Scott while you were away. It turned out the lawsuit was a mistake. Her son had filed on her behalf and she was more than happy to sign papers absolving Stella Sociedad and partners of all negligence. She was very amusing about it all."

"Her son?"

"*Si*, he is a lawyer. Not a good one, according to his mother." Natalia laughed.

Carlos felt disoriented. "How old is Senora Scott?"

"*Uno momento*, I will see." Natalia trotted back to her desk, her fashionable heels clicking lightly on the stone flooring. She promptly returned with a file folder and ran her white-tipped fingernail down a paper. "Lilith Scott, resident New York City, age fifty-six, a professor at NYU and a published author—anything else?"

"No, *gracias*." He took the folder and signaled her dismissal with a wave of his hand. He shook his head as soon as she closed the door behind her. What the hell did it mean? And who was the *Americana* in the Dominican Republic? He should have nipped this propaganda nightmare in the bud.

A few attempts at Google and he found a picture of Lilith Scott. She was an attractive, if oddly attired, middle-aged lady with bright red hair. Certainly she bore no resemblance to the young woman who had stolen her identity. How had the girl fooled the airline? More likely she had paid her own way and just fooled him. Putting aside the Lilith Scott file, Carlos focused on the other documents requiring his attention. A business meeting in New York suddenly seemed more appealing as he realized he could simultaneously sort out the identity of his conniving lover and determine her game.

*

The deadbolt opened with a clunk followed by the less impressive clicks and scrapes of the five remaining locks. Lily waited while her aunt struggled with the last sticky bar.

"There. I have it. You may now enter my fortress." Aunt Lilith gestured expansively, bringing attention to her cast now decorated in bright neon swirls. "I wish Lawrence weren't so paranoid. It drives me nuts living in a cage."

"So why don't you just tell him no?" Lily asked. "You have a doorman and it's a secure building."

"He wants me to be safe. As a lawyer, he hears about all these awful crimes in New York and projects those worries onto me.

I should be glad my son cares." Aunt Lilith took a step closer and peered at Lily's face. "Goodness dear, you look terrible." She hugged her and then backed up with a frown. "And you're too thin. Didn't they feed you at that resort?"

"They did. The food was fabulous. I must've picked up a bug on the flight home."

"Why didn't you call me? I would've run over with some chicken soup." She put her arm around Lily and steered her to the kitchen. "I'll make you a sandwich and you can tell me all about your adventure. And what about that hunk you mentioned? Did you see him again after the dinner? I've been dying to hear the rest of the story."

"Not much to tell. He turned out to be a jerk." She pointed at a small reclining nude on the hall table. "Hey, this is a new statue."

"No. I got it last year. Lily?"

"Oh. It's really nice. I love the Italian marble." The tears were threatening again. Lily searched her aunt's cluttered apartment for something, *anything*, to take her mind off Carlos.

"What happened, sweetie?" Aunt Lilith turned Lily to face her,

The last of her strength crumbled. "He th-thought I was a-a—prostitute," Lily gasped out between sobs.

Aunt Lilith let out a huff of indignation. "Who could possibly think that?" She grabbed Lily in a one-armed hug and awkwardly patted her back. "Oh, my poor baby."

"He seemed so nice. He taught me to ride and dance. I thought he liked me. Then he turned mean, like he had a split personality." Lily pulled a crumpled tissue out of her pocket and blew her nose. "Sorry. I wasn't going to tell you. You gave me this vacation and I turned it into a…" She turned away trying to compose herself.

"Don't be silly. It's not your fault." Her aunt's voice was soft but she could hear the anger underneath.

"I must be doing something wrong to attract only abusive guys. I should've known. He was so handsome and charming. No one that great would like someone like me."

"One day you'll meet the perfect guy, Lily. Trust me." Aunt Lilith smiled. "But you may have to kiss a lot of frogs before you find him."

Lily shook her head sadly. "I think I'll pass."

"Well, in the meantime, I'll make you a sandwich."

"I'm not hungry."

"You'll eat and you will enjoy," her aunt ordered, popping two slices of bread into the toaster. "And how is school going?"

"It's okay." Lily sniffled. "I'm a little behind."

"Because of the trip?"

"No. This new girl, Anna, turned up in class, and she keeps asking for my help. I ended up working on her armature for her sculpture and showing her around, but she just doesn't seem to be getting it."

"Can't you tell her you need to finish your own work?" Aunt Lilith held up a jar of mustard.

"No thanks, just mayo." she shrugged. "I know. I should tell her but I feel sorry for her. She's very lonely and needy. She told me her husband hits her."

Aunt Lilith plunked the finished sandwich down in front of Lily. "After all you went through with Danny, you're probably one of the few people who can empathize with how difficult it is to leave an abuser."

"Yeah. It took me two trips to the hospital and that persistent cop before I finally got out. And without you taking me in, I don't know—" Lily took a bite of the sandwich, surprised at how hungry she was.

"Did you tell her that?"

"Some of it. She asks a lot of questions, but, I guess because English is her second language, sometimes I think she doesn't really understand."

"Where is she from?"

"Spain. Which is also weird. She keeps asking about the Dominican Republic. I sorta mentioned Carlos, the Spanish jerk

I met, and no matter how often I correct her, she still seems to think he was the abusive one."

"Well, as long as she understands that she shouldn't go back to her husband."

"I think she got that part. I told her about all my broken bones." Lily shuddered remembering that last ambulance ride to the hospital. Even as they were trying to save her life, she'd still been defending Danny.

"There you go. Your experience has helped someone else avoid that heartache."

"I hope so. Anyway, Aunt Lilith, I've got to run, but I'll drop by next week if you're free."

"Anytime, sweetie." She handed Lily a banana from the fruit bowl. "And don't forget to eat."

The sound of her aunt re-latching all the locks on her door followed Lily all the way to the elevator. As soon as she stepped out on the street, the depression engulfed her like a soggy quilt. Why couldn't she return to how she felt before she'd met Carlos? Somehow, she kept coming back to how loved and accepted she'd felt when she was with him. Now here she was outside of society again with her nose pressed up against the window. It hadn't bothered her before she fell for him; now, the loneliness was unbearable.

*

On the subway ride home after a movie with Anna, Lily contemplated her new friend's parting comments about Carlos.

He can only be so bad because he is so rich. But you cannot let him speak last. And if he is rich, he is easy to find on internet.

The more she thought about it, the less absurd the idea seemed. Maybe e-mailing and telling him off would bring her closure. By the time she got home and turned on her computer, Lily was wired with anticipation. The name Carlos Diego pulled up over 75,000 results on Google, but when she added Barcelona she got him on the first hit.

Holy crap! He was some kind of celebrity. She scrolled down looking for information in English. When she got to the pictures of Carlos, she was shocked to see several of him with her on vacation. She hadn't noticed any photographers. The other women he'd been photographed with were all gorgeous models. Why the heck had he bothered with her?

After reading several articles, she began to appreciate the full scope of his identity. *A buyer indeed. He was a billionaire business mogul. God! Everything he said was a lie and I was stupid enough to believe him.* She spent over an hour surfing different sites until she found an e-mail address that appeared to go directly to him. After numerous attempts at getting the right tone, Lily sat back to read her final version.

Mr. Diego,

I have come to realize that you are an arrogant and deceitful jerk. Your decision to play with my emotions (and obviously I'm not the first female you have abused in this way) leads me to believe you have some unresolved Oedipal complex that causes you to hate women. You should consider psychotherapy before you do real harm to some poor female who actually falls for your macho bullshit.

Wishing you a speedy recovery,
Lily Scott

A surge of satisfaction suffused her as she hit send. A little Freud went a long way, she thought smugly.

*

The tabloids were getting worse. Somehow, they had found some hospital shots of Lily, or whatever her name was, and made it look like he'd beaten her. He'd insisted his lawyers sue *El Primo* for a retraction, but the small article indicating that the abuse pictures were from seven years ago did little to dispel the damage to his reputation. Then they printed several pictures of Lily's bruised calf at the resort, implying that was his doing. And Elena, ever the opportunist, was now insinuating he'd roughed her up as well.

Carlos buzzed the intercom. "Natalia, I'm going to New York for a week on Tuesday. Book me into the Hilton. Coordinate a meeting with the Tivali Group. Call Gianfranco to track down the reporter Anna Gomez from *El Primo*. Her byline is from New York. He is to locate her without tipping her off. And send him the pictures of the woman from the tabloids. Let's see if he can get an ID for her."

"Right away."

He should've sorted this out last week before it escalated, but he'd been occupied with the environmentalists. He finally solved their complaints and now a new scandal jumped in to fill the vacuum. Odd the mystery woman wasn't suing him yet. Maybe she preferred raking in the money anonymously from the tabloids. *El Primo* seemed to be receiving fresh gossip daily. Perhaps she was waiting for the nudie magazines to offer millions. A surge of arousal hit Carlos as he pictured Lily naked on his bed. She could make a lot of cash with that innocent face of hers.

He closed his computer and locked away his files. He was not going to work anymore today. A quick trip to his mother in the country and he'd formulate his plans for his New York visit. He had no doubt his security team could locate the *Americana*, but how he would deal with her, he did not know.

*

Carlos's penthouse suite overlooked Broadway to the east and Eighth Avenue to the west. The south windows displayed the darker back streets that made uptown Manhattan less appealing. It was still incredibly expensive real estate, but there was something inherently grubby about the black iron gates on the storefronts and the incessant, filthy steam wafting up from below the street. He watched dark clad pedestrians scurry like rats between the honking herds of taxis. New Yorkers were depressing in their damp grayness.

Usually he enjoyed Manhattan, reveling in the energy that simmered just below the conscious level. He always caught the new shows, tried the hot restaurants, and generally wondered why he didn't return more often. This time he was struck by the city's bleakness. Or was the desolation inside him?

*

Sitting in the darkened theater, Carlos felt decidedly underwhelmed by the phony posturing on stage although his date appeared to be enjoying the show. A surreptitious glance at the others in their box confirmed their approval. He was probably suffering from jet lag, he surmised glumly, although he felt more irritated than tired.

During an extended burst of applause, he smiled warmly at Dianne. She was very beautiful, yet he was trying to guess which parts of her were natural. Her forehead seemed immobile, but her striking almond-shaped eyes appeared unaltered. Her jaw line was strong. He hadn't decided if it had been enhanced. Her full bosom was delectable, but seemed artificially high and lacking any jiggle. Of course, some of that may have been due to her ridiculous couture. Her breasts squeezed out the top of her gown like party balloons about to pop. He sighed. He used to be able to simply enjoy a beautiful woman. *Why am I now so eager to find their flaws?*

"She sings beautifully, does she not?" he murmured in Dianne's ear.

"Yes. And she has such an incredible range." She placed her hand on his knee as if to emphasize her point. Her hand remained and when she raised her eyes to his, the invitation was unmistakable.

Carlos smiled in return. She might be the answer to his restlessness of late. He slipped his arm comfortably around her shoulders to confirm the deal. She whispered something about the costumes, her hand moving up his thigh. It made the last act a little more interesting.

Finally, the show ended with the obligatory standing ovations. Carlos was surprised to find his mind returning to Lily's enthusiastic applause for the amateur production at the resort. In a way, her response seemed more honest. No, he reminded himself, nothing about that woman was honest.

*

Back at his suite, Carlos poured Dianne a glass of champagne. She was admiring the view as he came up behind her with the drink.

"Ah Dianne, you look enchanting," Carlos murmured, nuzzling her neck. She arched back into his embrace. He raised his free palm to her breast and her breath caught as if in surprise. She turned to him, languidly moistening her lips with her tongue. Her kiss was decisive and her tongue dueled smoothly with his own. Her thigh pressing urgently against his groin was soon replaced by her hand.

After placing the champagne glass on the window ledge, he thrust his hand beneath her skirt to find her moist and accommodating. His fingers soon brought her to a quivering state but, despite his arousal, she was not the one he wanted. With a harsh expletive, he pushed away her grasping fingers.

"I am sorry, but not tonight," he said through gritted teeth.

"That's fine. Maybe you like to watch? I have a friend…" Dianne offered with a seductive smile.

"*No gracias.*" Carlos studied her more closely, wondering how swiftly he could remove her from his suite. "I am rather jet-lagged."

"Of course, airplanes can be tiring. Maybe some other time?" she suggested. His annoyance increased with her attempt to soothe his ego.

"That would be lovely. If I have time available later on…" He steered her toward the door.

"My number." Dianne handed him her business card and gathered her coat. "I'd enjoy seeing you again."

Carlos closed the door behind her, letting out a huff of exasperation as he read the discreetly worded card. He should've known his "date" was a professional. What was shocking was that he was uninterested in mindless sex. His mind went back to his phony *Americana*. She was his problem. His drive had been squelched by her betrayal; she'd been hovering on the edge of his mind all evening. Somehow, he needed to finish this whole tawdry business before he could move on.

*

"*¡Si!* Get on with it," Carlos barked at Gianfranco's man slouching in an ill-fitted suit in Carlos's penthouse suite. Why did American P.I.s feel they had to dress like slobs to do their job? Carlos knew Gianfranco paid his operatives well for their discretion.

"Sure, Mac. Your dough. This broad was almost too easy. Lily Scott, born in Springfield, Oregon, twenty-seven yea—"

"That *is* her real name?"

"Yup. You want the rest?" He shot Carlos an insolent look before flipping back through his frayed spiral notebook.

Carlos held his anger in check.

"No brothers or sisters, alcoholic mother, couple of stepfathers. Mother died leaving her on the street at seventeen. Worked a series of dead end jobs. Caught shoplifting. Hooked up with a bum, Danny Harmon. Police called twice to his apartment for disturbing the peace. She was hospitalized the last time, but wouldn't press charges. Moved to New York six years ago and seems to have kept her nose clean ever since. Lived briefly with her aunt in Manhattan and now has a bachelor suite in Brooklyn. Studies at The Art Students League on Fifty-seventh Street. No current boyfriend. Does massage therapy, but from the variety of clients, I would guess it ain't sexual. I couldn't get an appointment." He snapped his book shut and stared at Carlos expectantly.

"You are sure you have the right woman?"

"Of course. I squared it with the photos. She's a good-looking broad for all that crap." The man's leer made Carlos want to punch him. Instead, he handed over a couple of hundreds for a tip.

"Thank you for your work."

"My pleasure." With a casual wave, the man was on his way.

Carlos pondered the new information. Was Lily hired by someone because of her name? Or—he suddenly remembered her mentioning her aunt. Could her aunt be Lilith Scott, the older woman who'd tripped in the gallery? *¡Dios mio!* What if Lily hadn't been playing him? His stomach plummeted as he recalled his last cruel treatment of her.

No. She wasn't an innocent. There were still the photos and the tabloid leaks. Those had to be from her. But all the other stuff she'd told him was apparently true.

Carlos poured himself a Scotch from the bar. Knowing Lily was probably at her art school only a couple of minutes away was distracting. But according to the P.I., the tabloid journalist from *El Primo* was also at the school, so he'd have to proceed with caution. Could the reporter have tricked Lily? No, now he was just reaching for straws to justify the fact that he still wanted Lily so badly. His phoned vibrated and he glanced briefly at the message. A smile hovered on his lips as he realized who it was from.

Chapter Seven

Lily logged on to her Hot Mail site with reluctance.

"He won't reply to my message," she told Anna as she waited for her friend's iPad to respond.

"Rich men always have the last word." Anna sneered. "He will answer. You will see."

"Oh my God. You're right." Her hands felt instantly clammy as she saw her inbox. A message from Carlos R. Diego, subject: Before Psychotherapy. Was he making fun of her? Somehow just his name on the computer set her heart racing again.

"Open it," Anna urged her.

"I can't." Lily handed the iPad back to her friend. "I'm not going to let him have the last word. I just won't read it."

"That is *stupido*. He won't know you didn't read it." Anna touched the screen. "I'll tell you what he says."

"No."

"Ms. Scott. Please join me at the Russian Tea Room Thursday, Feb. 17 at 2:15. Sincerely, Carlos Diego."

"What? You're making that up." Lily grabbed the tablet from Anna and read it for herself. "Shit. That's tomorrow." She leaned against the gray cement wall and reread the short missive. Why?

"This is good." Anna smiled as she took back her iPad. "Now you tell him face to face what a bastard he is. I will go with you."

"I'm not going. I have work to do here."

"You go if I have to drag you there myself."

"No. And if I do go, it will be by myself." There was no way she'd let Carlos humiliate her in front of Anna. "Besides," she told her friend, "you have your anatomy class, and you can't afford to miss any more of those."

*

"Ooof!" Lily slammed the sculpting clay onto the board. There was something so satisfying about throwing large hunks of muck onto the table to beat the air out of it. The damp clay emitted an earthy smell, more soothing than most air fresheners. She had been working it for almost an hour; her arms ached, her back protested incessantly, but she felt better than she had for days. She didn't even have to picture Carlos's face on the table anymore. The exertion alone helped relieve her stress.

She glanced at the alarm clock perched perilously on the filing cabinet. Nearly two o'clock. Only a few minutes before she needed to clean up and meet Carlos at The Russian Tea Room. It was close to the League but trust Carlos to suggest such an expensive place. Well, she would make sure he paid for it, one way or another.

She hadn't planned to go to the restaurant but Anna had all but begged her to change her mind. Otherwise, he'd think she was afraid of him, her new friend had argued. Well, Lily wasn't afraid because he couldn't hurt her any more. Yes, it had been awful the first few weeks. She'd vacillated between hating his cruelty and craving the warm sense of belonging he'd created before his nasty transformation. Today she was definitely over him.

She straightened her shoulders, then gave one final smack to the clay. She didn't need a man to make her feel good about herself. As soon as she became a real artist, then she'd fit in. Men were way more trouble than they were worth. And odds were Carlos wouldn't even show up, being such a conceited big-wig. Instead, she'd meet some flunky sent to warn her off or threaten a lawsuit.

Even so, Lily still had battled with herself not to bring a nice outfit to change into. No make-up and just clay-covered sweatshirt and jeans. That should show how little she cared about his opinion. Lily smiled as she wrapped her clay in wet rags and cleaned her table. She hoped he'd be dressed in one of his fancy suits. In fact, she should arrive a little late.

*

Lily passed The Russian Tea Room frequently, but actually walking through the wobbly revolving door felt strange. If she hadn't been so pissed off at Carlos, she would've been intimidated by the maître d's snooty attitude. Instead, it felt good as Lily carefully intoned that she was there to meet Mr. Diego. A shocked expression briefly displaced the glare before his face settled back into his default air of condescension. His barely perceptible nod indicated she should follow him. Lily wished she could rub some of her clay splatter onto the man's red brocaded jacket. *No, keep all of your hostilities for the real jerk.*

The plush scarlet walls, dark wood, and elaborate décor all added to the hushed aura of money. An ornate brass samovar with delicate etching stood on the highly polished bar and then was reflected in the beveled mirrors behind. Unfortunately, the dim red table lamps made it difficult to identify the few afternoon customers nursing their drinks. Squinting, she scanned each face hoping to glimpse Carlos before he saw her. The tension between her shoulder blades built as she tried to maintain her casual composure. They turned a sharp corner and there he was, impeccably attired in a dark suit with a forest green, presumably silk, shirt. Lily had almost forgotten he was that handsome.

A rush of conflicting emotions flooded her as she valiantly fought to appear aloof. She remembered his every touch and its effect on her body, while at the same time his last vile words ricocheted to the forefront of her brain. Maybe this was what a female praying mantis felt? He seemed different, but that was probably because she knew his true character.

"Lily." Carlos stood immediately when he saw her. His eyes bore into hers, barely registering her casual, muddied appearance. "Thank you for coming." He pulled out a chair for her, dismissing the hovering maître d'.

"Carlos. Gosh, thanks for inviting me," she answered with as much sarcasm as she could muster. She would've preferred to sit opposite him, but wasn't quick enough to avoid the chair he offered.

"Lily, I'm sorry."

"What?" She'd worked through the many things he might say to her, but she hadn't anticipated an apology. Not that he didn't owe her one.

"I was wrong about you. I hurt you, and I'm truly sorry."

She regarded him closer and realized what was different. He didn't appear so sure of himself. Was this some kind of trick?

"Mind telling me why?"

"I panicked. You had come to mean too much to me too soon. I could not believe you were real." Carlos nodded to the waiter as he delivered his wine. "What will you have?"

"Coffee, please." Lily managed a terse smile for the waiter. "Now, wait a second. You're saying when you like someone, you attack them for getting too close?"

"No, not usually. Prior to meeting you, my fiancée cheated on me. I was becoming attached to you but suddenly I could not trust my instincts. I did not wish to be hurt again, so I said those horrible things."

Lily opened her mouth to respond, then snapped it shut.

The waiter placed her coffee before her and walked several steps back to the kitchen before she remembered to call out, "Thank you."

"*Bella.* I am a suspicious man. Because of my position, many people try to take advantage." Carlos lifted her hand to his lips and she steeled herself against the surge of longing that swept through her. "Words cannot convey the depth of my sorrow."

His warm brown eyes enthralled her despite her best efforts. "But…"

"Lily, you are different from the people I normally meet."

"You mean gullible and stupid?" Lily snatched her hand away. Her senses momentarily regained, she determined that her best defense to keep from being fooled again was to avoid his eyes and his touch.

"No, open and honest. I did not trust because it was too fast. I was wrong. I want you back in my life. Please."

"What?" She stood up, stunned. "No…I mean, this is just… weird. You said terrible, unforgivable things. How would I know you wouldn't turn mean again?"

"But Lily—"

"No. Goodbye, Carlos." She turned to leave, desperate to make a clean escape, but her bag tipped over her coffee. "Oh God, I'm sorry." Throwing a napkin on the spreading puddle, she bolted for the door. Her face burned with embarrassment and too many other emotions to account for.

*

"Oh God, Aunt Lilith." Lily waited in the hall, fidgeting with her canvas bag as her aunt struggled with the last lock. "I shoulda left things as they were. Now I'm even more confused."

"Oh damn." Aunt Lilith reached down quickly to retrieve her dropped cigarette. The glowing embers were the same shade as the lipstick smear on the other end. "Tell me what happened."

"It was bad." Lily groaned in frustration. "He apologized."

"Wasn't that what you wanted, dear?" The vibrant scarf tying back Aunt Lilith's hair shimmered as she shook her head in confusion.

"Uh huh. Then he said he wanted to see me again."

"Did you tell him to go self-masturbate?"

"To do what? Oh, yeah. I guess I did." Lily walked into the kitchen and opened a cupboard. "Do you have any chocolate milk powder?"

"Behind the cornstarch. Why are you confused, Lily?"

"I still want him. I mean how sick is that? Didn't I learn anything from my first rotten relationship?" The cupboard door closed louder than she anticipated and she jumped.

Aunt Lilith watched Lily pour the chocolate powder into a glass and handed her a spoon. "Did he say why he'd insulted you?"

"Some crap about how his ex-fiancée had cheated on him, so he got scared," Lily scoffed, stirring in the milk. The clink of her spoon against the glass grated on her nerves.

"And you don't believe him."

"Would you?" Lily gave up trying to get the lumps out of her drink and took a chewy sip. "I just can't believe he thought I would take him back."

"Well, good for you for giving him what-for." Aunt Lilith paused and looked skeptically at her niece. "But now you're having second thoughts?"

"I can't help it," Lily groaned. "When Carlos was nice, he was the most incredible man I ever knew. I have never felt so good about myself, so beautiful, so happy, as that week I spent with him. Will I ever feel that way again?"

"Sure you will. There are plenty of fish out there."

"But I've never met anyone like him before."

"Okay, Lily. Back up, sweetie. I'm confused. Do you want me to tell you it's okay to date this guy again? Because if you think he really is sorry and won't hurt you again, then go for it, kiddo. All I want is for you to be happy."

"That's the problem. I know I can't trust him. And anyway, it couldn't be a real relationship because he still lives a million miles away. But when I saw him, and he looked at me that way, I don't know…I would've put my hand through molten steel to be with him again."

"Hmm." Aunt Lilith gently rubbed Lily's shoulder. "What are you going to do?"

"I guess nothing. I mean, I told him I wouldn't go back to him, so that's it. Abusive guys can't change overnight. I've already made that mistake once. I'm not sure about anything, these days, but I think maybe I'm learning."

"Good. Now how about eating something a little better for your poor stomach? I have some lentil soup I can heat up."

"No, thanks. I can't stay. I'm on my way back to school. Thanks for listening, Aunt Lilith."

"Anytime, sweetie. You know I'm here. Locked in my gilded cage." Aunt Lilith picked up a Balducci's Deli bag from beside the door. "Here, I got you something for later. No. Take it. If I can't get you the occasional treat…"

"Thank you, Aunt Lilith. But honestly, I do eat okay on my own."

*

Lily got within a block of the school before her curiosity got the better of her and she opened the little boxes in the bag. The top box was from the bakery and contained a piece of cheesecake, a chocolate cannoli, and a profiterole. The second box was fancy cheeses and smoked meats. *There certainly was no fear of becoming anorexic with Aunt Lilith around.*

The rest of the afternoon dissipated in fits and starts. Immersed in her work, the time would fly by. Then thoughts of Carlos would bombard her brain and everything slowed to an annoying crawl. By the time her class was over, Lily barely resisted the urge to run screaming from the school. Instead, she made her usual way back home.

There was no message from Carlos on her phone, nor on her e-mail. Good. That was it. He'd apologized, been rejected, and probably was flying back to Spain. She sighed. Unless he still had business in New York.

Lily dipped into her aunt's treats while she thought about it. *He wouldn't have flown to New York just to see me.* Yet that possibility had hovered at the back of her mind all day. And why had he waited four weeks before apologizing? Did her e-mail shame him into it? *Oh God. This is insane! Why can't I just forget about him, once and for all?*

*

Carlos stood by the railing watching the horses being saddled. Aqueduct Racetrack was one of the few places he could truly lose himself in New York. It was remarkably nondescript as far as racetracks went. A large, mostly empty, grandstand towered behind him. The paddock was a ten-foot drop below him, surrounded by heavy poured concrete and metal railings. Out of the small saddling stalls, the horses danced nervously around a small patch of grass waiting for the signal.

The other patrons were indistinguishable from the crowds you'd see at almost any racetrack around the world; the slightly seedy older men scribbling notes in their crumpled racing forms; the younger swaggering men, eager to boast of their previous winnings; and the various immigrant groups clumped in different sections.

The steward shouted, "Riders up!" and the trainers hoisted the small jockeys in bright silks aboard their mounts. The magnificent animals turned once more in the paddock and then trotted onto the track. This was a longer race at a mile and a half, which meant the horses were loaded and started right in front of the crowd. So much of a race was won or lost in the brief moment the gates opened.

Carlos strode to the fence to watch the parade to the post. Lily would love these beautiful thoroughbreds. He imagined her smile and excitement as she watched the mounts with their ears pricked forward and dancing in anticipation behind the gate waiting to be loaded.

This was also the most dangerous part of a race. The horses were well trained in starting from the mechanical gates, but sometimes one would shy up at the noise and excitement. A ton of crazed animal, large metal beams in every direction, and a one-hundred pound jockey trying to control the situation was a disaster waiting to happen. It was a testament to the skill of the trainers, jockeys, and starting gate crew that there wasn't a constant flow of blood at the start of every race.

Carlos sighed with relief as the fourth horse, Commander N Chief, loaded without incident into position. The horse had been previously barred from racing in Saratoga for bad gate behavior. The bell rang, metal gates crashed open, horses surged forward with a thundering of hooves, and the race was on. Carlos admired the way the jockeys curled up to meld into the flowing muscles of their mounts. Their faces tucked into their horse's neck, arms on either side steering and encouraging the steed. A vision of Lily laughing as she galloped her horse over the beach in the Dominican Republic rose in his mind and he pushed it aside.

Carlos jogged back to the finish line to get a better perspective as the horses crossed for the second and final time. The race took less than three minutes, but in that time, so many hopes and dreams were realized or lost. This was still early in the racing year, so the purses weren't large and the field was less famous. But to the horse's owners, it meant as much for a thirty-five hundred dollar claimer to hit the winner's circle as if they were competing for the millions in the Triple Crown and Breeder's Cup races later in the year.

The chestnut filly Carlos had chosen led for most of the race but got passed in the home stretch. He threw his losing ticket in the garbage and focused on the next set of runners. It was a baby race—two year olds, most of whom had never run before. They were enchanting to watch, like skittish teenagers growing into their long, skinny legs. Lily would've adored them. But they weren't worth betting on, as there wasn't enough information to even guess as to how they would run.

Somehow the novelty of being back at the track had worn off. His mind turned fully to his problem with Lily. He hadn't considered that she'd turn him down. Especially when he could tell she was still attracted to him. Perhaps she needed time before she would accept his apology. Fair enough. He had a few more days of meetings in New York. He would give her some time to come around.

With a last glance at the eager colts nervously eyeing all the unfamiliar sights and sounds, Carlos returned to his limo. No point in second guessing the future. He needed Lily now, both to restore his reputation and for his physical well-being. Mostly the latter, he smiled, recalling her sweet face gazing up at him from the sheets. He wanted her back in his life and back in his bed.

Chapter Eight

Lily let herself into the apartment and dropped her bag of groceries onto her coffee table. An apple rolled out onto the floor and she ignored it, slumping onto the futon couch. She hadn't felt so tired for weeks. *This is frigging Carlos's fault.* She'd just gotten over him, well mostly, and then the jerk turned up again.

It was over and yet somehow that ten-minute meeting had set her back to dreaming of him again. At least today she hadn't run to check her computer to see if he'd tried to contact her. Mostly because she was too exhausted. Lily hugged her pillow and lay down on the couch. A nap and then she'd be productive.

A sharp rap on her apartment door wrenched Lily out of a fitful sleep. Her watch said it was only seven o'clock, so she quietly went to the door and peeked through the peephole. Sighing, she opened the door.

"Hi. What's up?" Lily's building superintendent was nice but often overly conscientious. She'd been very careful sorting her recycling since his last visit.

"You were out. Man came to deliver this." Gregor handed her a brown bag and turned to go.

"Wait. It's not for me. I didn't order anything."

"Yes. Is for you. Your name is on card." Gregor opened the bag and pointed at a white envelope inside before disappearing down the corridor.

A rush of optimism that it might be from Carlos swept over her, then a wave of guilt at her lack of willpower. Either way, she didn't want to look at the card. Nevertheless, she took it out of the bag. No, the writing didn't look like Aunt Lilith's. Lily peeked inside the bag again and found a takeout food container. Maybe her aunt had phoned in the order and the restaurant wrote her name and address on the envelope.

She opened the box and let out a little gasp of surprise. The chocolate dessert looked remarkably familiar. How could Carlos have gotten it here from the Dominican Republic? Reluctantly she opened the envelope and read the letter.

Mi Angelita,

I would do anything if I could only take back the pain I caused you. Once Tony suggested that countries could not be at war if they were eating his Chocolate Amore. I am hoping the same can be true of us. We were good together and I promise we can be again. Please agree to have dinner with me tomorrow and I ensure you will never regret giving me a second chance. I long to hold you in my arms again and make up for the grief I have caused you. I will call for you at six-thirty.

Tu Amor Siempre,
Carlos Diego

Lily covered her mouth with her hand. *Damn him!* He knew all the buttons to push. And, damn her for wanting to believe him. Crumpling the letter, she stomped into the kitchen, heading for the garbage can. No. She shook her head. She couldn't throw them out. She tossed the dessert in the fridge and flattened out the letter.

Should she go out with him again? Now that she knew he possessed a cruel side, she could guard her heart against him. It would be a physical hook-up, nothing more. Her pulse sped up. And at the first whiff of any negative aura from Carlos, she would high-tail it out of his life. Then it would be her choice to end it—well, sort of.

Lily smiled as she continued to mull it over. If she went out with him in New York, it would also be easier to get away if the date turned bad. And if it went well… Her body was already humming in anticipation.

*

At six-thirty, Carlos buzzed the intercom outside Lily's apartment. Brooklyn was definitely a part of New York he was unfamiliar with. The soot-darkened buildings had a decrepit look that spoke of years of neglect and subconscious anger. The garbage and recycling bins lining the sidewalk had been rifled through for any potential profits and now spilled casually onto the curb. One of the gray piles of material on the cement moved and a grubby hand pulled a beaten blanket in closer. Carlos glanced over his shoulder at his shiny black limo, his driver sitting even more stiff-backed than usual inside.

There were several people about, but would anyone intervene if his driver was carjacked? Even bodyguards were vulnerable to high-powered weaponry. Or was he reading more malevolence than existed into the blackened windows and grubby homeless figures?

"Yes, who is it?" Lily's voice was barely discernible over the intercom's crackling.

He was pleased she answered. He'd worried she'd try one more power play and ignore him. "It is Carlos."

"Second floor. C'mon up." The intercom screeched to unlock the door.

The lobby was clean, but after looking at the aged and graffiti-scratched elevator, Carlos took the stairs. Although they were equally unappealing with a disgusting odor, at least there was no worry about them breaking down.

He rearranged the bouquet of orchids and then stepped out into the second floor hallway. Midway down, a door stood open and he saw Lily watching the other way for the elevator. He paused to admire her sleek silhouette. She was dressed simply in black pants and a black sweater. Her ebony hair curled casually down her back. Carlos strode up behind her, the faded taupe carpet muting the sound of his footsteps.

"*¡Hola!* Lily." He smiled when she jumped at his voice.

"How did you—? The stairs, sorry. Let me just lock up." She slung a light coat over her arm and started to close the door.

"Perhaps you should put these in a vase first." He handed her the flowers.

"Oh. Thanks... Do you want to come in for a second?" She didn't sound too thrilled with the idea.

"*Gracias.*" Carlos surveyed the apartment with interest. The incredibly small living room was dominated by a futon couch and an old computer on the coffee table. A narrow passageway led to the kitchen and a closed door, presumably to the washroom. Where was her bedroom? Maybe there was another room off the kitchen.

Several odd unframed pictures competed for the scant real estate. A garish collage with various naked body parts overpowered a rather dull still-life. A minimalist abstract in oil was marginally better. While Lily was in the kitchen with the flowers, he examined the paintings closer. Thank God, they weren't signed by Lily. Some sculptures peeked out from behind the couch with a ratty towel partially covering them. Those must be hers.

"So where are we going?" Lily returned before he could examine the various lumps. Despite her casual demeanor, her hands shook as she cleared the small table and placed a plastic juice container with his flowers beside the computer.

"Paramour. The new restaurant by Robert d'Ange."

"Oh, is it French?"

"*Sí,* he is known in Paris. The food should be good." He smiled at the understatement. His effort to impress her with an impossible-to-get reservation had gone unnoticed.

"Okay. Well, let's go. I've been hurling clay all day; I'm starving." Lily's speech was as hurried as her movements as she rushed into the hallway.

"Hurling clay?" He followed and watched her systematically lock her door from top to bottom. How could she live in such a dangerous area? And what, aside from the amazing sex, could he have in common with someone who lived like this? And yet even as he considered the disparity in their lives, he had to admit she fascinated him. She was a different creature here on her home ground. Less malleable, more sassy.

He placed his hand on the small of her back as they entered the rickety elevator. He wanted a lot more contact, but knew he had to be patient. Still, he couldn't prevent his hand from curling around her waist and was shocked to feel her hipbone jutting out. She had been a lot softer in many ways in the Dominican Republic.

*

Lily stood frozen in the old elevator, willing herself not to respond to Carlos's touch. Even this small contact was driving her crazy. She wanted to throw herself into his arms and lose herself in his kisses.

"Did…" She cleared her throat and started again. "Did you have any trouble finding where I live?"

"No. Finding a decent florist in this neighborhood, now that was difficult." His smile reminded her of the time he'd teased her about her Ping-Pong coaching in the Dominican Republic. The elevator bumped to a stop at the main level and, after some consideration, let them exit. On the street, he pointed to a limo, double parked and ready for a quick get-away. "My car is there."

As they neared the vehicle, the driver jumped out and opened the passenger door for them. She slid across the seat making room for Carlos before realizing he'd already claimed the seat opposite.

Great, now it looked like she was trying to sit as far away from him as possible.

"I don't bite," he told her with a smile.

"Good. I wouldn't want to spoil your appetite." Oh God, where had that come from? She was supposed to be playing it cool, not flirting with him. "So where is this restaurant?"

"Off Times Square. And because it is French, you will not have to worry about wasting food. A good French restaurant always leaves you hungry for more."

"Well, here we could ask for doggy bags and give them to street people. I'm always in the wrong place at the wrong time."

"No. You are exactly where you should be." Carlos shifted to the seat beside her and raised her fingers to his lips. "Lily, you look enchanting tonight."

She snatched back her hand then pretended it was because her wrist itched. How could this man affect her so deeply with so little effort? One kiss sent her pulse racing. A gentle waft of his unique scent invaded her nose, sending all sorts of sensual memories coursing through her body. She wanted to bury her face in the crook of his neck where she remembered the hint of vanilla and sandalwood had been strongest.

She turned to watch the traffic on the bridge. It seemed safer. A bus roared by, its passengers trying to peer through the darkened windows of the limo, probably hoping to see a celebrity. After composing herself mentally, she looked back at him.

"So how long are you in New York?"

"I have a meeting here next Wednesday if all goes to plan."

"And then you're back to Barcelona?"

"I will see."

As much as she wanted Carlos, seeing him again didn't make any sense. Surely he knew that, too. On vacation she had imagined them visiting each other. Not likely. A day or two once or twice a year when he was here on business seemed too weird. Together they watched the changing views in silence as the driver pushed through the uptown traffic. Finally, the car stopped in front of a carpeted walkway.

"Do not be alarmed by the photographers," Carlos advised her. "Just smile and keep walking."

"Photographers?" She didn't have time to say any more before Carlos offered her a hand out of the limo. A blinding flash disoriented her and she was thankful when he pulled her close to his body.

"Carlos Diego! *¡Aquí!*"

"They know who you are?" Lily asked, amazed.

"The restaurant would have given out the reservation list for publicity. They are hoping for real celebrities. Just in case, they'll take our pictures."

"*¿Donde esta Elena?*" a short man shouted as the rest of the paparazzi rushed off to crowd around the next limousine.

"*Sin comentarios,*" Carlos answered with a smile and then guided Lily into the restaurant.

Inside, the bedlam was of a different nature. Servers were flying through the crowded tables with controlled efficiency, their platters held high, their faces plastered with obsequious smiles. Conversations were animated and punctuated with over-exuberant laughter. And many of the outrageous dresses women were wearing wouldn't have looked out of place on a fashion runway. She was way underdressed. Luckily everyone seemed too busy to notice, as they performed to an unknown but important audience.

Carlos handed their coats to a hovering attendant and they followed the maître d' to their table. The other diners glanced to see if they were anyone before quickly focusing on the next group entering the restaurant. Their table was in the back corner where it seemed there might be a hope of a conversation.

"What did that man yell at you outside?" she asked once they were seated.

"*Nada.* Nothing of importance. They try to get you to look at them to improve their photo. I am sorry. I did not realize this restaurant would be so hectic."

She raised her eyebrows. "You knew to expect photographers."

"*Si.* Robert D'Ange is a famous chef. He would not open without—hoopla? Is that the correct word?"

"I guess so. Oh my God. Is that Robert De Niro over there?"

"Probably."

"This is so weird. I—" Lily cut herself off as she saw the waiter approach.

"*Bon soir.* Welcome to Paramour. My name is Henri, and I will be your server. We have a special just for tonight—*tout gout*, a taste of all. It is a shared platter and I highly recommend it. Here are your menus. Your sommelier will be along soon. Shall I give you a few moments to decide?" At Carlos's nod, the waiter gave a slight bow and withdrew gracefully.

"Would you like to try the '*tout gout*'?"

"Um…sure." Lily absent-mindedly chewed her bottom lip.

"Do not look so worried. It will not be all snails and frogs' legs," Carlos chided her.

A diminutive gray-haired man with an air of distinction introduced himself as their sommelier. Lily listened in surprise as he and Carlos conversed in rapid fire French. After the man left their table, Carlos turned back to her.

"Excuse my rudeness. I did not think you cared to join in a conversation on the merits of wine."

"How many languages do you speak?"

"Four passably. Several of my dealings are in France and Japan, and you cannot command respect if you cannot communicate."

"Oh." God, what was she doing here with this man? Their waiter returned and she watched as Carlos ordered their meal. When the man left, she asked, "So why didn't you order that in French?"

"I'm not certain our friend Henri actually speaks French and I did not wish to embarrass him."

A light buzzing emanated from her purse. "Excuse me a moment." She dug out her phone and turned it off. "Sorry."

"*Bueno.* Now it is just the two of us." His eyes commanded her attention as he leaned in closer. "*Bella*, I was not totally honest about myself when we met. I am sorry. I am a cautious man with strangers out of necessity. I should have trusted you. Anything you wish to know now?" He smiled sheepishly.

"I figured out you weren't a buyer when I got home and Googled you. What do you do?"

"I am a fortunate businessman. I made various investments in my early days and parlayed the wealth into a vast company that dabbles in many different interests. The majority of my dealings are in the shipping industry."

"Oh." She ran her finger along the moisture gathering on the outside of her water glass. "The articles didn't mention, are you married or anything?" She held her breath.

"No."

"Divorced? Kids? Mistresses?" Lily sipped her water and considered her options. Was she committing to something just by asking him these questions? Carlos was not a man she dared toy with. If he knew she was hooked, he wouldn't let her back off again. But did she want to back off? She blushed recalling how wonderful he'd made her feel in bed. She had slept with him before, knowing it was a dead end relationship. This time at least she would have a clearer vision before jumping in.

"I was affianced to Elena Corrina. I am no longer," he admitted. "No children, no mistresses—at present." The heated look he gave her left no doubt as to his meaning.

"Ah," was all Lily could manage. The waiter returned with their food and she was thankful for the diversion.

Carlos helped her to several dishes, explaining what they were as he doled them out. Squid and octopus were added to her "too yucky to try" list but there was still plenty of other delicious food. They ate in silence for a few moments before she had to ask.

"Is Elena Corrina that super-model who does all the work for kids with AIDS in Africa?"

He nodded noncommittally.

"She's amazing. I saw her on a fundraising program and she seemed so nice. Was she the—?" Lily choked as she remembered him saying his fiancée cheated on him. "Oh God, I'm sorry. That's none of my business. She is very beautiful," she couldn't help adding.

"Yes. What about you? Any boyfriends or children I should know about?"

"No. I don't really have time between work and school."

"It is important to have time for love." His eyes held her with their intensity. "Without *amor*, there is no life."

"There's always chocolate," she countered nervously. One look and her entire body tingled with desire.

"True. Still for me…" He raised her hand to his lips and kissed her palm. "This is much better."

Lily's mouth went dry and she gulped some water. If only she could dump the rest of the glass over her head to cool down. She needed to change the topic, and fast. "I think maybe your theory about French restaurants is wrong. I'm pretty full."

"It is difficult to find a good theory," he agreed with a low chuckle. He caught the waiter's attention.

Henri appeared at their table instantly. "May I clear these dishes?" he asked. "And would you care for coffee and dessert?"

"Not for me, thanks."

"*Non, merci*, Henri." Carlos passed him his credit card before Lily even realized he had reached for it. Luckily she hadn't planned on chipping in for the meal. An awkward silence enveloped them while they waited for Henri's return.

"Thank you for—"

"Would you like—?"

Lily smiled, embarrassed. It used to be so effortless with Carlos. "Ah, *merci,* Henri." Carlos signed the proffered bill and pocketed his card. "Shall we?"

They stood and Carlos's hand on her elbow sent electric currents scorching through her body. It would be so easy to give in to her desire. But it was equally obvious how incredibly mismatched they were. She wasn't going to want to let him go again. Then how badly would he have to insult her a second time?

As they shuffled into the line for their coats, she noticed the crowd waiting to enter had grown considerably. The photographers and reporters were no longer evident. Either they had deadlines or else no one else famous was expected.

"Excuse me, Miss." A man carrying two full-length fur coats pushed in front of her. Stepping back, Lily's spine came up against Carlos. She was about to move ahead when two more people followed the man through the new opening. Carlos's hands held her shoulders, steadying her. Without thinking, she leaned into his chest. His arm instantly circled her waist holding her firmly against him. She froze while she considered her options.

The line suddenly surged forward and Lily moved to the side as Carlos presented the tickets. Lily assumed an air of nonchalance as he helped her on with her coat. His hand rested on the small of her back as they walked into the chilly night air. Outside he paged his driver.

"He'll be a few minutes. Are you warm enough, *bella?*"

"I'm a little cold. Any ideas on how we could warm up?" Lily asked with a nervous smile and inched a step closer.

*

Carlos's smile widened as he drew her into his embrace. He'd hoped he could entice her back. She was different from his previous women; he hadn't been sure.

"*Sí*. The cold is a problem I can fix." Carlos folded his arms around her, kissing her temple and working his way down until he found her lips. It was like coming home as she opened up to him. Her tongue teased him, promising and then retreating. He shifted slightly and her body melted seamlessly into his own. When he bent to kiss her earlobe the dark mass of his limo rolling up to the curb caught his attention. A quick squeeze, then he helped her into the car and slid in beside her. "Will you come to my place?"

Lily paused and Carlos held his breath. "That would be good," she finally answered.

After giving the driver instructions, Carlos closed the privacy window. He threaded his fingers through her hair and pulled her face to his for another searing kiss. His hand worked its way under her sweater to stroke the soft skin at her waist. She didn't stop him. She quivered in anticipation as his fingers feathered up her rib cage. A gasp rewarded him when his thumb gently caressed her breast through her bra. The limo stopped and Carlos fought to regain his self-control.

"We are here," he said needlessly.

They walked swiftly through the ornate lobby to the elevator. Once inside the mirrored lift he held her. He dared not do more. If he started he wasn't sure he could stop. The elevator opened to his private suite and he kissed her hungrily.

She broke free immediately and her eyes widened with surprise. "Oh my God! This place is huge. Is this all yours?"

"*Sí*, of course. Would you enjoy a tour?" Carlos covered his reluctance with a polite smile.

"Um, yeah…"

Carlos sensed Lily's hesitation seeping back in. Taking her coat, he led her to the window before she could bolt. "There is Broadway in all her glory." He kissed her neck as she gazed out at the brightly lit buildings screaming for attention. "Through there is my washroom, and this is my bedroom." He deliberately turned her to face him and caressed her cheek with his palm. "*Bella?*"

Lily reached up and pulled his face down to meet hers. His control shattered. The feel of her soft lips under his only made him want more. He needed to taste her neck just below the earlobe. He needed to feel her flesh against his own. Lily seemed equally driven as she ripped open his shirt to press her lips to his chest. He groaned in response to her tongue teasing his nipple. They shed their clothes hastily and barely made it to the bed before she cried out to him, "Hurry. Please hurry, Carlos."

Pausing only for a condom, he dove into her sweet warmth, her beautiful legs curling around his hips. If only he could sustain this feeling forever—but the excitement drove him further and faster into her. She threw her head back in ecstasy, her hips rolling up to meet his. Nothing existed other than the building sensation pulling him into her. She crunched forward in climax, her inner muscles shuddering around him. He groaned in response; his final thrusts poured into her.

His arms shook as he held himself above her staring at her flushed face. How could this woman have so much power over him? He had never experienced such animalistic sex. There was no finesse, no seduction, just a raw need for each other that overrode every other emotion. And yet it had been perfect.

*

Lily lay in the vast hotel bed trying to regain her wits. When had she turned into this crazed sex addict? She knew Carlos was an amazing lover but she'd never thought she could be that uninhibited. Had she actually screamed for him to take her?

Oh God, next week he'll be back in Barcelona and I'll be going through the heartbreak all over again. And can I cope with being his

New York mistress, knowing he'll probably soon have another mistress back home?

Lily lowered her eyelids trying to stem her flood of thoughts. *Enjoy the moment and deal with tomorrow when it comes.* She opened her eyes to see Carlos standing over the bed staring at her. He seemed to be memorizing every detail of her body, the heat of his scrutiny burning her until all her nerves hummed in anticipation.

She let her gaze slide slowly down his flawless body, drinking in the tanned muscular shoulders, the chest with the swirls of hair, down to the taut abdomen. A pale scar near his hipbone drew her eye. She continued her appraisal stopping when she reached his impressive erection. She glanced up at his face to see the desire mirrored there. He climbed back onto the bed beside her and Lily held her breath.

"This time I will treasure every inch of your glorious body," he murmured in her ear. He kissed his way down her neck. His lips, his tongue and the scratchiness of his five o'clock shadow created a myriad of physical sensations. Meanwhile his hands roamed her already sensitized body, molding and stroking her flesh with precision.

She was on fire, each caress igniting the flames of her passion. A gentle kiss to the inside of her ankle, a single finger stroking behind her knee, and finally his tongue licking her core. It was like an out-of-body experience as she writhed under his touch. How could he know exactly where and how to touch her so deeply? She pushed him away and onto his back. His surprised expression changed to one of anticipation when she covered his body with her own.

"Now you are mine," she whispered and she began her exploration. She licked and stroked her way down his torso. It was amazing to have someone react so instantly to her every action. She'd never felt so powerful or sexy. Carlos's breath was ragged.

How long would his control last? His beautiful body vibrated with tension.

Carlos wordlessly handed her a condom and she covered him. They shared a languid kiss while she lowered herself onto him. The sensation of him filling her was tantalizing. His hands gripped her waist and he plunged still deeper inside. She lifted herself until they were barely connected and then slid down, the electricity building between them.

Lily lost all semblance of control when she heard his guttural cry. She answered him with her body, consuming him. After, she melted onto him in an exhausted heap. His fingers gently swept back the hair that had fallen to conceal her face.

"*Dios*, Lily."

She looked up at him questioningly. He merely smiled and kissed the top of her head. She dropped her head back onto his chest, his heart pounding in her ear. She wished they could stay like this forever.

*

Carlos lightly stroked Lily's silky skin as she lay across his body as if she was made for him. Exciting while making love and in the afterglow she fit perfectly in his arms. Could he be in love? No. Even though he'd been wrong in his accusations in the Dominican Republic, he did not know her. But he'd never had such a compelling need for someone. Her fingers traced circles on his chest, the calluses on her thumb tickling him. Reluctantly he slid out from underneath her.

"*Uno momento, mi angelita.*"

He needed some distance from her. He needed to think. He was prepared to admit he was infatuated with her but that was all. Still he couldn't go home without her. There wasn't much holding her here. She could fly back to visit her aunt. She wouldn't miss that tiny apartment. He could buy her a fully equipped studio and take her to art galleries around the world. That'd be more beneficial than any classes. And she wouldn't need to do massages or sell any of her artwork; he would give her anything she wanted.

Excitement bubbled up inside him. Such a simple solution. He would insist on some sort of pre-nup when she moved in. *No problema.* He could certainly afford to be generous when they parted.

Carlos quietly padded back to the bed. He wanted to tell her his plans but when he looked at her peacefully sleeping, he couldn't bring himself to wake her. He spooned up behind her warmth and covered them both with the blankets. A kiss on her shoulder caused her to cuddle more snugly against him with a sigh.

Chapter Nine

Lily's eyes flew open and she scanned the unfamiliar room. When she noticed Carlos's tanned hand resting on her waist, the previous evening flooded into her sleep-addled brain.

Oh God! What have I done?

It'd been wonderful but what if he woke up and told her he'd slept with her just to prove she was a tart? She couldn't bear the rejection. Not again. Could she sneak out without waking him? As if suspecting her thoughts, Carlos sleepily pulled her tighter into his embrace. She searched the room for a clue as to the time.

It was Thursday, so she had a class at nine o'clock. She still had to get home, shower and change clothes before she went in. Black clothes were not a good idea when working with clay. Hell, good clothes were not a good idea with clay. She spotted her watch lying on the floor beside the bed.

When did I take that off? She stretched out to grab it.

Oh shit! Eight o'clock. She'd have to bust her butt to get to Brooklyn and back into town in time. Could she ask him for cab fare home? That seemed so cheap and sleazy but the alternative of being late for class didn't thrill her either. Her pants would survive if she didn't do any welding, but clay would probably ruin both her shoes and sweater.

Carlos's hands began a slow reconnaissance of her body and she realized he was waking up.

Lily turned to face him. "Hey. I've got to hurry. My class starts in an hour and I've got to go home first to change." Maybe he'd be nice and offer her a ride.

"No, you can stay a while. *No problemo.*"

She peeled his roving hands away and ran for the bathroom. She'd shower here and save a little time. He grumbled something in Spanish from the bed. He was obviously not going to be any help.

Inside the bathroom, she halted in her tracks. It was incredible. The shower was bigger than her whole bathroom with several showerheads to shoot water from different heights and angles. Too bad she didn't have time to enjoy it. With a little guesswork, she managed to turn on one showerhead. She picked up the soap, then turned at the sound of the catch on the shower door releasing. Carlos stepped inside the shower to join her, his towering frame instantly filling the oversized enclosure. His early morning facial hair gave him a rakish appeal. And damn, his body was beautiful. She didn't realize she'd dropped the soap until she heard the echo of it bouncing on the enamel floor. Bending down to pick it up, she collected her thoughts. *Shower, school, hurry.* She couldn't allow herself to be distracted.

"I have a good idea. Why don't you come back to Spain with me?" He took the soap from her and began to lather her body.

"What?"

"We will fly today." He lifted her hair to drop a scratchy kiss on her neck. "You will love Barcelona."

"But I have class…" Lily sputtered.

"You can miss one class. We will fly back to New York next week." He leaned into her and his lips gently pulled on her earlobe while his breath sent chills down her spine. She couldn't think when he did that. Plus his hands were still roaming freely over her sudsy skin.

"I have a massage client tomorrow and two more on, um… Tuesday." She struggled to recall her schedule. Her brain was not cooperating. "And a class show on…Thursday. My piece has to be mounted and ready by Wednesday."

"Cancel tomorrow and I'll have you back on Monday."

"But—"

"*Por favor, bella.*" His lips found hers and she was unable to resist.

"You promise I'll be back in time?" she asked breathlessly.

"*Si*. Come back to bed. We will leave at ten."

Lily gave up thinking as he tantalized her body with increasing urgency.

*

At nine, after polishing off a sumptuous breakfast, Carlos was on the phone arranging for their flight.

"But what about my clothes? I need to get home to pack a few things."

"We will buy everything you need there. Do not worry. There are very good stores in Barcelona. Victoria Beckham and other celebrities often go there to shop."

"But my—"

"No buts. We will visit your apartment to get your passport and toothbrush, but no time to pack." Carlos added with a beseeching smile, "Allow me to show off my city's modern style."

Lily nodded; it was churlish of her to complain if he was willing to buy her new things.

Her mind spiraled in all directions as she finished drying and brushing her hair. This was insane. But what if this was love? She backed off from that thought with alarm. *Don't go brainless here.* Carlos had never said, "I love you." and flying her to Barcelona might not be a big deal to him because he was so rich. Maybe it was the equivalent of someone at the League springing for dinner at Nobu; more effort than taking you to a pub, but not love and marriage time. A discreet knock on the bathroom door yanked her out of her thoughts.

"Lily, the driver will be here in ten minutes." He smiled as she came out. "Ah *bueno*. You will fall in love with Barcelona, *mi amor*."

"I'd better call my client...oh, and my aunt." She scrounged in her purse for her phone and went into the other room. She left a message for the client and then phoned Aunt Lilith.

"Are you sure you want to go, Lily? Barcelona is beautiful, but if you have any doubts about this man…"

"I don't know, Aunt Lilith. I mean, we had the most amazing night and he really does seem sorry about what he said. Then again, I'm still not sure I can trust him." She heard Carlos barking orders into his BlackBerry in the other room. "But if I don't go, I'll always wonder. Does that make sense?"

"You know me, dear. I'm always a sucker for a romantic ending. Or even just a romantic weekend. Hell, at my age—" Lilith chuckled and then her voice turned serious. "But listen, if anything goes wrong, you call me collect at any hour. I'll wire a plane ticket and money to you in an instant."

"I'm sure I'll be fine."

"I mean it, Lily. Hopefully everything will be great, and you'll have a marvelous time, but remember, I'm here if you need me."

"Thanks. You're the best."

"I know. I'm the best aunt you've ever had. Have fun sweetie, and call me as soon as you're back."

*

Lily appeared anxious as they headed toward Carlos's private jet.

"Your visit will be perfect," he assured her. "My household staff in Barcelona are all fluent in English and will be at your beck and call. Maria runs the house. She is older and tends to be a little cheeky," he admitted with a grin. "My cook is Federico, and even if he feeds you well, you must not fall in love with him. He is married to a girl in the shops and I believe they are very happy. The rest you will meet in passing. As it is the weekend, the caretaker and gardener will not be there."

Yet she still seemed worried and tense.

They boarded the jet and he was rewarded by her bald enthusiasm for things he had long ago taken for granted. She bubbled with excitement as she took in the comfortable living room atmosphere inside the luxury aircraft.

"This doesn't look at all like a plane. Do we still have to wear seatbelts?"

"Only taking off and landing. It is a flight rule," he advised her. "The washroom is behind us. If you get hungry or bored, let me know. We have a fully stocked kitchen, movies, games, and computers, whatever your heart desires. What would you like?"

"How about a paper and pen?"

"A little low-tech, but I think I can find some." He nodded at a thin impeccably dressed woman standing by the cockpit door and relayed Lily's request. *Certainly easier to please than his previous flying companions.*

"You wish to write a letter?" Carlos asked when the writing pad was produced.

"Oh no. I was thinking about sketching." She glanced around. "So, where should we sit?"

He led her to the high backed chairs facing the movie screen. "We will be comfortable here until we hit altitude. Here is your seat belt."

The captain emerged from the cockpit and cleared his throat.

"*Señor Diego*, we have been cleared for takeoff. Flight conditions are good with a tailwind. We should arrive in Barcelona in just under seven hours."

"*Gracias.*" Carlos watched the man return to the cockpit before he turned to Lily.

"As soon as we are airborne, I will get you a drink." Carlos paused, then added, "Or anything else."

"Thank you. What do you normally do on these flights?"

"Work, I'm afraid. But I don't have to. We can talk, play games, watch movies, whatever you like."

"Can we have sex in the bathroom?" she asked with a mischievous grin.

"That would be very uncomfortable. Do you want to?"

"Well, isn't the Mile High Club where you have sex while flying?" Lily's face flushed a lovely shade of pink.

"There is a bedroom on the plane. We could make love in comfort if you'd like."

"Oh." She appeared to think about it. "If it's allowed, then I don't think it counts."

"Let me know if you change your mind," Carlos said with a chuckle. He kissed her palm and then held her hand for take-off. Despite her assurances, he wanted to make sure she wasn't afraid.

Chapter Ten

"*Bella*, we are here."

Lily jolted awake to the sound of Carlos's voice in her ear. *My God! I fell asleep on a plane.* She was becoming blasé. The last thing she remembered was Kate Winslet saying something about Paris. That must've been the movie.

The landing strip was coming in fast and she craned to see as much of the scenery as possible. With the tall buildings and bright lights, Barcelona at night seemed much more like New York than her hometown of Springfield.

"She is pretty, no?" Carlos murmured in her ear.

"Yes," she exclaimed.

"We will sleep in my apartment tonight. Tomorrow we will shop for everything you require. And then we'll go to my house in the country. It is further out but I hope you will like it."

"I'm sure I will," she answered. "Hey, do you have horses?"

"No, unfortunately." His wistful tone made Lily wonder, but he didn't explain.

The jet landed and taxied to a small hangar and she heard men yelling in Spanish. The captain eventually emerged to inform them they could exit. She stopped to pick up the mess they had made in the previously pristine jet, but Carlos dissuaded her.

"We pay people for maintenance, do not concern yourself."

*

The quick drive from the airport to Carlos's apartment was pretty much a blur of city lights and advertising sandwiched between quieter neighborhoods where it appeared much of the city had gone to sleep. Their limo pulled up to an old stone building not unlike many of the condo buildings in uptown Manhattan.

Inside the lobby, the tiled floor and brass fittings gleamed. Carlos said something in Spanish to the elderly doorman and then ushered her into an old-fashioned elevator. As he closed the ornate wrought-iron doors, a sense of dread overtook her. She was miles from home where nobody spoke English and she was totally dependent on Carlos. If he turned cruel again, she'd be trapped. How could she have agreed to this trip?

No. Lily closed her eyes and reasoned with herself. She could call Aunt Lilith at any time. Lily concentrated on her breathing and releasing her body's tension.

"Lily? Are you all right?" Carlos searched her face, his eyebrows furrowed with concern.

"I'm fine." She rubbed her eyes. "Probably shouldn't have napped on the plane."

"We'll have a snack before bed. That may help. The time change is difficult sometimes." The elevator creaked to a halt and Carlos directed her down the hallway. "My apartment is not ornate," he warned her as he unlocked and opened the door. "I use it when I work late and do not wish to drive home."

Lily glanced around the living room with curiosity. Much like Carlos's suite in the Dominican Republic, there didn't seem to be anything personal to indicate that he had ever been there. "You could use some sculptures," she joked, "but other than that it seems nice."

"This is not where I entertain," he reiterated. "Let's see what food my assistant left for us."

Lily followed him into the fair-sized kitchen. Despite the age of the building, everything inside looked new, spotless and rather unfriendly.

Carlos pulled a platter of cold cuts and cheeses out of the fridge and gave her an apologetic look. "I hope this is fine. I eat lightly before bed."

"Great." She sat on the bar stool he indicated and watched as he brought out cloth napkins and small plates. He was as considerate and caring as before but something had changed in her. She couldn't shake her feeling of vulnerability.

The meal progressed like a strange movie. Carlos was talkative and charming but she found herself not really listening and responding. He seemed to accept that her distraction was due to jet-lag.

After their snack, he showed her through the spacious apartment. It was like walking through a furniture showroom or a very clean hotel. The sterility of the place made her even more aware of how little she knew this man. It was a relief to have a moment alone in the bathroom to prepare for bed.

She slid under the covers while he brushed his teeth and took some deep, relaxing breaths.

The bed dipped to the other side as Carlos lowered onto it. He shifted to spoon against her. Then he raised himself onto his elbow and looked at her face.

"Lily, what is wrong?"

"Nothing."

"Are you angry with me?"

"No. I…" She couldn't explain what she didn't understand herself. "I'm very tired."

"You don't want to be touched?" He sounded confused.

"No." She held her breath.

A moment passed, then he kissed her forehead and rolled away and onto his back. "Buenas noches, mi amor."

"Good night." Lily turned onto her stomach and buried her face in her pillow. She shouldn't have come to Barcelona.

*

Her pillow smelt odd. Lavender? It was a soothing scent that reminded Lily of her nice grade two teacher. She cracked a sleep-encrusted eyelid open and peered cautiously around her. Carlos was not lying next to her; this probably was Barcelona; and damn she could really use a few more hours of real sleep. She closed her eyes again but knew she wasn't going to get any more rest.

With a stifled groan she sat up in the massive bed. At least she wasn't as worried this morning. She rarely got anxiety attacks these days and at least now they didn't last very long. Grabbing a long white t-shirt out of Carlos's bureau, Lily trotted to the bathroom to clean up. God, her face was pale, and she had a lovely crease mark on her cheek from the sheet. She scrubbed her face with a cold cloth and headed out to find Carlos.

He looked up from a newspaper as she entered the kitchen, his smile broadening when he saw her wearing his shirt. "Buenos dias, Lily. I didn't like to wake you this morning, you looked so tired." He held open his arms and she slipped gratefully into his embrace.

"Morning," she murmured, her face buried comfortably in his soft sweatshirt. "What time is it?"

"Eight-thirty, which is half past three in New York." He kissed the top of her head before releasing her to pour her a cup coffee.

"I guess that's why I'm turned around." Lily hopped onto the stool beside him and leaned over to kiss his cheek. It was smooth, he'd obviously just shaved. Had he been up for long waiting for her? "So what's the schedule?"

"Today we will go out for breakfast, then shop before the stores close for lunch. After that, we go to my home where you can relax. We will do tourist things tomorrow."

*

Tears lurked behind Lily's tired eyes as the bossy store clerk sternly measured her every body part. The morning had started off well with a fabulous breakfast of coffee and pastries. Then they had spent too long and too much money at the drug store with Carlos determinedly buying fancy shampoos, conditioners, and a variety of "personal care" items that she wasn't even sure what they were for. Now they were in a designer dress shop looking at ridiculous evening gowns. But how could she say anything without seeming ungrateful as Carlos continued to pull out his damned credit card at the least provocation?

She'd thought when he'd said they'd buy stuff for her visit that she'd get a four pack of undies, a pair of jeans, and a couple of t-shirts. The fancy lingerie the woman had piled on the counter looked like dry clean only and none too comfortable. It would be fun to have one set of sexy underwear to wear for Carlos, but mostly she preferred to have actual material between her and her jeans. And jeans also seemed to be a far cry from Carlos's mind.

"*¡Aqui tienes!*" The woman handed her a floor length blue gown with crystal beading emphasizing the low cut bodice. "*Este.*" Next came a red taffeta number with a frightful number of frills. "*Y tambien.*" Then a slinky, black, one-shouldered affair you couldn't possibly wear with a bra.

She took the three gowns into the change room, hastily closing the door so the woman couldn't follow her in. The blue dress looked way too big so she tried it first, the faster to discard it. Sure enough it hung like a gaudy, static-charged shower curtain. The red one fit better but looked more appropriate for a homicidal bridesmaid. She reluctantly modeled it for Carlos.

"It is not you?" he asked with a sympathetic smile.

"No. These frills look silly."

Carlos began speaking to the woman in Spanish while gesturing at the dress. Lily slipped back into the dressing room. The black dress was stunning, clinging to her body like a second skin. Perfect for a fashion model, but she couldn't imagine wearing it without tripping on the train or accidently exposing herself. She slunk out of the dressing room.

"*Bella*, that is beautiful." The look of hunger in his eyes worried her. Fine if it were only for him, but what if he wanted her to wear it in public? And wouldn't the long train get filthy if she walked anywhere?

"It's a little tight," she offered quietly.

"*Dios, no. ¡Perfecto!*"

Lily changed back into her black pants and sweater and brought the three gowns out to hand to the woman.

"The blue one?" he asked.

"It was way too big," she told him, glad to have a legitimate excuse.

He nodded and handed his card to the woman with another torrent of Spanish. She slumped in the chair by the door.

"What is it, Lily? I thought all women loved shopping."

"Oh, I really appreciate it all. Thank you. It's just I'm tired. *Gracias!*" she called out to the woman who was scribbling on her order pad.

"*Bueno.*" He seemed pleased with her feeble attempt at Spanish. "You will be sounding native in no time." He led her back out into the street. "What else would you like?"

"Maybe some cheap sweats, just for, you know, wearing around." Lily's face burned with embarrassment. She hated asking but she did need something other than the clothes she'd been wearing for two days straight.

"Of course you need other clothes."

She heaved a sigh of relief and looked up the street with renewed interest. *La Plaça Catalunga.* It was beautiful with cobblestone sidewalks and ancient brick buildings. The shops inside the old buildings however, were all very modern. Carlos propelled her to a younger store filled with jeans, t-shirts and casual wear. They were greeted by a woman who looked like a younger Penelope Cruz. Were Spanish women all that naturally beautiful?

"Choose what you like. You are size thirty-six?"

"Is that an eight?" She hadn't realized the sizes would be different.

Carlos discussed with the clerk and then replied, "Eight would be thirty-eight."

Lily picked a pair of jeans, a long sleeved t-shirt and a zippered sweater. "I'll try these on," she called out, waving the clothes at the young clerk. She walked toward the dressing room and then had to wait for the woman to unlock the door.

"¿Tres?"

Lily nodded hoping the woman wouldn't ask her anything else. If only she'd studied the Spanish language ads on the subway back home. The clothes fit pretty well. Did she have to model them for Carlos? It seemed only polite since he was buying them. She trooped out to see him conversing animatedly with the clerk. She felt awkward interrupting their conversation.

"Is this okay?"

"¿Que?" He eyed her clothes. "Si. But try this, too." He handed her pile of clothes with a knowing glance at the saleswoman.

Lily squelched the pang of jealousy that shot through her and threw on the new selections. She was overreacting but she didn't want to leave him alone with that woman any longer than necessary. The new clothes were great, too. She wasn't sure which to get.

"Muy bonito. We will take them all."

"But..." She didn't know whether it was good or bad that she didn't know how much the clothes cost. From the look of the store, they probably weren't cheap. She changed back into her clothes and joined him at the cash register as he pocketed his card. She shook her head at the absurdity of the day.

"What is the matter? You do not like the clothes?"

"No. They're lovely," she explained. "It's just so strange to be here with you paying for everything."

"And this is bad?" His head tilted in confusion.

"No, not bad. Just weird. But I really appreciate it. I mean, don't get me wrong." Lily could tell he didn't understand. "So that's all the shopping for me. Do you need anything?"

"You are buying?" he asked with a smile.

"No, I mean…you know what I mean." She groaned with exasperation.

"I am teasing." He drew her in for a hug. "Let us go to my house and I'll show you around." The mischievous look in his eye worried her.

*

They drove through the city and Carlos pointed out various tourist attractions. Lily loved Antoni Gaudi's unfinished church of *La Sagrada Familia.* He'd have to bring her back for a tour of the church when they were less tired. And she said the men playing bocce in the park reminded her of the Village in New York.

It was a relief to see her enthusiasm return. He'd never met such a reluctant shopper, especially when he was picking up the bills. Well, she'd get used to it. Obviously, she could never afford to dress appropriately on her own.

Carlos smiled as he pulled Lily in closer to kiss her forehead.

"Good grief! What is that building?"

"That is *La Torre Agbar.* Also known as 'The Suppository'—"

"The what?"

"The Suppository. Like the pill you place…" He faltered. "It has a few other names, equally crude. They have many lights on at night and it is beautiful. But it is an unfortunate shape. It was finished in 2004 and is head office for a water company."

"Oh." She was silent for a while. "I think I prefer the older architecture."

"*Si.* But the new ones make the old ones look better in comparison."

"I guess. So why don't you have horses?"

"They are too much work. I would not have enough time to concentrate on business."

"But couldn't you hire people to look after them?"

Carlos sighed. "I would not wish to. Grooming, feeding, and exercising are all expressions of love to your horse. Why would I have an animal that would love another more?"

"I thought you were rich enough that you could let someone else run your company."

"No!" He was appalled at her suggestion. "I have built this business up from the soil. To let someone else direct her, it would be *loco.*"

"I'm sorry. I didn't mean to offend you. But you'd seemed so happy riding in the Dominican Republic—"

"That was vacation. I have responsibilities, to the families who work for me and to my shareholders."

"I guess so. And if that makes you happy…"

"It is not a matter of happy." Carlos shook his head at her lack of comprehension. It was, perhaps, an American concept, happiness regardless of duty. He changed the subject. "We are coming to my house on the left."

The car drove through a cobblestoned driveway lined with graceful old chestnut trees. A final turn revealed a gray stone mansion. Lily's face lit up in appreciation.

"This is your place?" She leaped out of the car to admire the building. "Look at the masonry. This is beautiful. And the engraved crest by the door is your family crest, I take it."

"It is from the original family that lived here."

He smiled at her first impressions. Usually women noticed the vast size of the building, the rolling green countryside overlooking the Mediterranean Sea, or even the four-car garage housing his luxury cars. Lily was trying to guess the age and significance of the grinning gargoyles hovering from the eaves.

"They are so much more animal-like than most of the ones you see in New York. There seem to be three styles."

"They are for protection, and they do a good job."

"I am going to love painting—" Lily stopped mid-sentence.

"What?"

"Nothing. I guess we should grab our stuff from the car so your driver can take off."

"He will wait for us," Carlos chided her.

"I know, but…" She slung her winter coat over one arm, purse and newly acquired pad and paper in the other hand. "It feels weird not having any luggage. And why wouldn't the stores let us take home our purchases? Do they have to wait to see if your card clears?"

"Delivery is a convenience here. I assure you my credit is good."

"Oh, I didn't mean…God, I keep jamming my foot in my mouth." Her face flushed. "At least we have the stuff from the drug store."

"*Si*," he agreed. "Now I will show you around. I must do some work from home today, but we will find many things to keep you amused."

Inside Lily's jaw dropped as she gazed around the foyer. "This is bigger than some hotel lobbies. And I guess this is real Italian marble. You're lucky I don't have my sculpting tools; I don't know if I could've resisted such beautiful stone."

"You will have to resist. I like my floor as it is. The drawing room." He opened the door then continued on with the tour. "My library. Feel free to borrow any books. Many are in English. This is my office. I also have a laptop upstairs you can use for the internet or whatever you like. The washroom. And through here," he opened the French doors with a flourish, "is the formal dining room."

She looked dazed at the size of the table.

"It seats twenty as it is. We can add more boards if required."

"And do you have these formal dinners very often?" Her voice was tinged with skepticism.

"I enjoy sharing good food and drink with friends. And occasionally I host for my employees and business partners. Now the kitchen. Come, you will meet Federico."

He took her hand and led her into the kitchen. Federico was kneading some pastry as they entered, with telltale white wires dangling from his ears. Carlos chuckled as he heard the tinny strains of hip hop music escaping. He tapped the chef's shoulder.

"*Buenas tardes*, Federico."

"*¡Ay caramba!*" Federico hastily stashed his headphones in his pocket.

"I would like to present Miss Lily Scott, Federico. She will be staying for a few days and is in dire need of proper Spanish food." Carlos winked at her.

"I am very pleased to meet you, Miss Lily," Federico bowed.

"*¿Encontada?*" Lily looked up at Carlos questioningly. He smiled and nodded. It was good she was attempting the language.

"And here is the dining room I use if I am not eating in my office." Carlos ushered her into the smaller sunroom. It overlooked a grove of olive trees shining in the sunset, the trees seeming to run in endless rows.

"It is for breakfast and lunch as well. Then we have the formal sitting room, mostly used for impressing heads of state," he joked. "And then up the stairs." He glanced at the fixed expression on her face. Was she already bored?

*

Lily tried to mentally shake herself as she followed Carlos up the grand, cherry wood staircase. It was like she'd stumbled into some old Merchant and Ivory film, or maybe more like that dream where you're somewhere prestigious and suddenly realize you're still wearing your ratty old pajamas or worse, naked. At any moment, she would do something incredibly embarrassing.

Meanwhile Carlos continued the tour as if this was a perfectly normal way of life. Well, she would enjoy her brief visit with Carlos, but it showed what she had known all along—this relationship was merely a brief affair. They passed a few guest bedrooms all decorated exquisitely, and then Carlos paused outside of one room.

"This is only temporary," he warned her.

Did he mean she shouldn't plan on moving in? *How rude!*

"Of course. Obviously, I have to go back on Monday," Lily responded hotly.

Carlos seemed puzzled by her response then opened the door. Lily was equally confused when she saw the room. She had expected more of the same bedroom furniture. Instead, there was a drafting table with drawing supplies facing out the large bedroom window. A heavy table was across the other wall with a box of clay. An easel with a blank canvas and what appeared to be two paint boxes were stashed against the third wall. Lily stared blankly at Carlos.

"I said I would make sure you had plenty to do," he said proudly. "When the rest comes we will move you into a different room. A larger one. I hope this will be sufficient for now."

"But…" Lily was dumbfounded. The art supplies were apparently new and still in their wrapping. *How had he…?*

"I want you to be happy here." Carlos wrapped his arms around her waist and pulled her back against his chest. "If there is anything else you need, just ask. The kiln will arrive next week but it will have to be in the shed because of the power requirements." He turned her to face him. "*Bella?*"

Lily searched his eyes. She'd only agreed to come back with him yesterday. This surprise must've been one of the many phone calls from his suite in New York.

"This is all too much, Carlos. Thank you."

Lily struggled to stem the tears welling up in her eyes. God, he'd think she was crazy if she started bawling now. Lily stood on her toes to kiss him. She felt so overwhelmed by everything in Barcelona, but when he kissed her back hungrily, her worries were temporarily allayed. In his arms, anything seemed possible. Lily let out a surprised laugh when Carlos suddenly swept her off her feet.

"Just imagine you have injured your leg," he told her with a smile as he carried her into the next room.

Lily nipped at his neck and kissed up to his earlobe. His arms tightened around her when she blew gently in his ear.

"You have put me under your spell, my beautiful witch." Carlos put her on the bed and covered her body with his own. "When I am near you I can think of nothing but your tempting body and all the wicked things I want to do to you."

"Mmm, sounds good," was all Lily managed to respond while encouraging his skillful plundering of her body.

Every time he touched her, he did something different that brought her to new heights of arousal. With a contented sigh, Lily shut out all her niggling doubts and succumbed to her desires. After the long sleepless night in his apartment, and the frustrating day shopping, her release was explosive. Carlos seemed more caught up as well, his face frozen in tension as he buried himself ever deeper inside her.

"*Dios*. Lily. *Mi. Amor.*" He gasped as he emptied into her. He rolled onto his back taking her with him. "I will not be able to work with you here."

"Okay," Lily answered with a kiss on his chest.

"Okay? That is your response as you bring down my company? You are a witch." Carlos was smiling. He brushed her hair away from her face. "I love your eyes. They are the summer sky at dusk with so much promise of the night to come."

"Um, thanks." Lily snuggled in closer to hide her expression.

Her heart had almost stopped when she thought he was going to say he loved her. God, what would that feel like?

If only they could stay in bed and never have to deal with the outside world. Was Carlos thinking the same thing as he held her close? He'd seemed disappointed when she hadn't been excited with the shopping trip. And her response to the house hadn't been right either. Should she have faked it? No. And first she'd have to figure out what he expected or hoped for. It would be easier to fake an orgasm, but at least that would never be necessary.

"*Mi angelita*, I must tear myself away to do business. But if you wish to rest more…"

"I think I'll take the watercolors outside. I'd love to take a whack at capturing those gargoyles."

"Whatever you wish—except for my flooring." Carlos bent over to kiss her. "I will find you in two hours for lunch. If you want for anything, just ask. Maria will bring your purchases when they arrive."

Lily stretched in the big bed after Carlos had gone. *Man, even the sheets feel rich. A person could get used to this way too fast.*

She glanced around the room with interest. The heavy, masculine, dark wood furniture, polished to a soft gleam, indicated this was Carlos's bedroom. The other bedrooms had been more neutral in tone.

Lily borrowed a bathrobe and began a closer inspection. A triptych of simple ink sketches of horses hung above the headboard of the vast bed. One other sketch of a cowboy with a lasso was on the wall opposite. An ornate trinket box was on the shorter of the two bureaus. For cufflinks and rings, Lily guessed. So far, she hadn't seen Carlos wear any jewelry but maybe he broke it out for his huge dinner parties. She peeked inside, then shut the box guiltily when she heard a low rap on the bedroom door. A short round woman bustled in laden with huge bags.

"Ello, jou must be Leelee. I jam Maria." The woman had an infectious smile and Lily responded instantly.

"*Buenos dias.* I'm pleased to meet you." Lily slowed down her own speech for the woman. "Can I help?"

Maria peered at her vaguely until Lily reached for one of the bags.

"Ah, *si. Gracias.*" She pointed to the closet. "*Allí.*"

Lily opened the bag to find it was the dreaded red dress, but as she looked closer, she realized the frills had been removed. She hung it up and picked another bag. It was the blue dress but again significantly altered. *My God, they worked fast.* Hopefully, they hadn't turned the black dress into a mini skirt, she thought as she took out the last one. Nope, it looked the same. Lily went back to find Maria putting away her new lingerie. Lily blushed, but it wasn't as though she could explain she didn't really wear things like that.

"*¡Muy bonita!*" Maria grinned, holding up a red lacy bra and panty set. Lily smiled and shrugged her shoulders. The rest of the clothes disappeared into drawers and then Maria turned back to her.

"Wel-come." A smile and a nod then Maria backed out the doorway.

Lily grabbed the least risqué underwear, new jeans and t-shirt and happily dressed. She was tempted to incinerate her black outfit, but presumably a good washing would suffice.

The art supplies made her mouth water. Watercolors, graphite, oil pastels, oils and each with the appropriate paper or canvas. The oils were BlockX and even included the expensive cadmiums and cobalts that she usually tried to stretch out due to the price. It was difficult to know where to start. She decided the watercolors would be best for the yellow/gray translucent tones of the old mansion.

*

A couple of hours later Carlos found Lily perched on an old stone wall doing ink and watercolors of his home.

"These are very charming," he commented looking over her shoulder. He was relieved he didn't have to lie. After seeing the questionable art works on her wall, he'd wondered if she had any artistic talent.

"Thanks. They're just the prelims. I think the end piece should be in oil. There's so much here I want to paint, it's overwhelming."

"I am glad you are happy. May I steal you away for lunch?"

"Sure. Let me clean up."

"Maria can get one of her girls—"

"No." Lily tried to explain, "I'm very picky about how paints should be put away. It won't take me long."

"If it pleases you."

"So was work good?"

"It never changes. We have a function tomorrow night, you and I. Roberto can no longer attend. It is at the Hotel Avenida Palace. I'd wanted to take you there for the architecture, so we'll kill two birds."

"What sort of function?"

"An awards event put on by the Santa Domingo Board of Trade. The awards will be dull but brief, and there will be drinks, dancing, and perhaps famous people." Carlos wondered why she looked more worried than excited. "I believe your gowns came today. Any one of them will be appropriate."

"Great." Lily smiled and picked up her paint supplies. "Well, shall we?"

Carlos followed her to the house. What was bothering her now? Elena had been difficult, but at least he'd understood her. Perhaps Lily worried about not having nice shoes?

"Do not worry about shoes, Lily. Natalia, my assistant, will bring several for you to try tomorrow. I told her your shoe size." Carlos pulled her to him and kissed the top of her head. "Everything will be fine," he reassured her.

Chapter Eleven

If it wasn't for the looming social event, the day would've been absolutely perfect. Waking up to Carlos's caresses, a delicious breakfast, an afternoon spent immersed in exotic scenery armed with her watercolors, Lily was in heaven. But at the back of her mind the thought of attending some snooty business function scared the heck out of her. She made her way back to the house to prepare for the evening.

She heard a loud squawk and craned to see a Monk parakeet looking down at her from an olive tree. Yesterday Carlos had shown her some of the estate, pointing out various birds and other wildlife. He'd almost convinced her that the parrots were indigenous to Spain, before admitting that they had been imported as pets. Then, as people had tired of their voices, they had been set free to crowd out the natural species.

"Yeah, same to you, buddy," Lily called out with a chuckle.

She wished she had more time before she had to get ready for the affair, but Carlos had made an appointment for her to have some sort of make-over. He seemed to think it would be a treat and she didn't want to disappoint him again. At least the woman was coming to the house so it wouldn't be as bad. Probably ten times as expensive though. *Stop worrying about how much all this costs. When in Barcelona…*

The woman was tall and gorgeous. Lily looked at her doubtfully as she walked around Lily inspecting "the project."

"Sit here. A facial." The woman indicated her face, in case Lily hadn't understood, "then *las manos*." She tapped Lily's hands. "Then make-up and dress. *¿Si?*"

"*Si.*" Lily nodded with what she hoped was enough enthusiasm.

Back when she'd first moved to New York, her aunt had taken her to an exclusive department store for a make-up demo, and it'd been awful. The woman there had been so enthusiastic about contouring her lines, thinning her nose, and bringing depth to her face, that by the end, Lily couldn't decide if she looked more like a hooker or a paint-by-numbers picture. Aunt Lilith, of course, had been enthralled with the results. Hopefully this woman was a lot more skilled.

*

It seemed like hours before the woman was putting the final touches on her make-up. Lily was wearing the long slinky black dress after deciding she would be less noticeable in black. Maybe she could say she was cold and wear her coat over it.

Lily smiled hopefully as the esthetician did one more critical circle around her. The woman reached in her bag and pulled out two half-moons of plastic and held them out to Lily.

With an exaggerated sigh of exasperation at Lily's lack of comprehension, the woman reached down the front of Lily's dress and stuck the plastic underneath one breast. Lily was so shocked she didn't react and suddenly the woman was propping up her other breast with plastic as well.

Then she sprayed some sort of sealant on her face and stood back to admire her handiwork.

"*Perfecto,*" she proclaimed.

She brought out a mirror for Lily. At least the thick foundation concealed Lily's furious blushing.

"*Gracias.*" Lily fought the urge to rub her face. It felt itchy and she was afraid to smile in case it all creased. And she looked so fake—well, maybe just not like herself.

The woman gathered her many pots and potions and stowed them in her giant rolling make-up bag. She strutted to the foyer with a confident familiarity.

"Tell Carlos 'ello," she said, sailing out the door.

Lily looked in the full-length mirror. The plastic bra things did make her appear bustier. But would they stay in place? Time would tell. And the nails, good God, they could be lethal. A low rap on the door drew her out of her thoughts. She turned to see Carlos standing in the doorway. His dark tuxedo emphasized his perfect physique.

"*Dios* Lily, you are a vision of beauty." He held her shoulders and carefully kissed the top of her head. "Do not worry. I have been well trained not to mess the face." He smiled. "After, I will not be restrained. Did you find some shoes to suit?"

"Yup. They're by the door. But you may have to walk slowly because I'm not good at heels." She looked at Carlos and asked her stupid question. "How do I keep the train from getting dirty?"

"You don't," he answered simply. "Your main concern will be if I step on it while dancing. I will be cautious. Are you ready?"

"As I'll ever be." She inhaled a deep breath and took his arm. At the door, she slipped into the heels and then stopped suddenly. "Oh. Can I take my coat?"

He looked at her like she was crazy.

"It will not be cold. We will be outside for only a moment."

When she slid into the car, the dress didn't shift down at all. Maybe the toupee tape would work. And hopefully she wouldn't have to walk far in the heels. She crossed her fingers surreptitiously.

*

It was like a replay of the French restaurant in New York with reporters hollering questions at Carlos as he propelled Lily along, shouting occasional answers. Although here he apparently was famous enough to hold their attention.

"*¿Quien esta su enamorada?*"

"*Sin comentarios.*" Carlos paused at the door and turned them both to smile and wave at the photographers.

"You are doing beautifully," he whispered as he guided her through the hotel entrance.

Once they got inside there were more press but these seemed more civilized. Lily was pleased Carlos kept a firm grip around her waist as they worked their way through the lobby. *And holy crap, what a massive lobby.*

Two ornate curving staircases began at either side and met above the hallway in a balcony. Every post, archway, banister was carved, gilded and shone within an inch of its life. The chandelier would've put the *Phantom of the Opera* to shame. And the floor tiling could've been hung at the Metropolitan Museum as a piece of art. Lily tried to refrain from gawking as Carlos led her through to the ballroom.

"Lily, this is Juan Perez. He is the chairman of the Santo Domingo Board of Trade and our host this evening. Juan, Lily Scott, a sculptor from New York."

"*Encontado.*" Lily wondered if she should nod, curtsey, or shake hands.

"*Encantado.*" The man bowed low and kissed her hand. "You are far more beautiful than any sculpture imaginable."

"Thank you." She laughed with embarrassment.

"Enjoy your evening." Senor Perez bowed again and left.

"We shall get a drink and then I'll show you around," Carlos informed her. "You will enjoy the art work; they have spared no expenses in this hotel." He smiled and nodded to several people they passed but did not stop.

Lily paused to admire a beautiful statue of a woman draped in a white toga, then jumped when the statue discreetly winked at her.

"Oh my God! She's amazing." Lily stared with renewed interest at the other statues. She had seen live mannequins in New York, but they were not nearly so detailed, right down to "cracks" in their marble skin. "How do they stay so still?" she marveled to Carlos.

"They are street performers. They do this for a living in Las Ramblas. The theme tonight is Business for Humanity. Stone to human. I am not explaining well, I fear."

"No, I get it." She gratefully sipped the ginger ale he handed her. Several cameras clicked behind them and she turned to see why. "Isn't that—?"

"Elena, yes." Carlos sounded less than pleased as he watched his ex-fiancée working the crowd. "I'd heard she was seeing the Minister of Trade."

"I'm sorry." Lily wondered by his response if he was still in love with Elena.

She certainly was gorgeous, even more stunning in person than on TV. Long golden tresses, classic face, more than abundant cleavage, a tiny waist and then the long shapely legs that went on forever. Lily wasn't a big fan of Elena's dress, though. She wore minimal skin-toned underwear barely covering the essentials, but everything else was showing through the sheer fabric pretending to be a gown. The photographers and every male save the professional statues were gaping in awe.

Lily glanced again at Carlos. He appeared more irritated than aroused. Or was he jealous of the other men crowding around his ex? Well he was here with her not Elena, Lily reminded herself as she casually took his arm. He smiled down at her and squeezed her hand in return.

"Come, let us find our seats. The speeches should start soon." He led her through the crowds. Sure enough, people started filing into the ballroom. Carlos pointed out a few people she might know.

"Rafael Nadar, the tennis star. He is now one of the top marketable figures in Barcelona. And the footballers are very profitable. Last year the Beckhams were here. Now they are more Hollywood than European, so their advertising power has shrunk. Tereza Toma, the actress." Carlos shrugged as he acknowledged her blank expression. "Sorry, no American stars."

"That's okay, the statues are way more interesting," she told him before the emcee called for silence.

Lily tried to keep an interested expression on her face as the main speaker enthralled the rest of the audience. She perked up when Elena's date, the Minister of Trade, rose to speak. He was an older man, not nearly as attractive as Carlos. Perhaps he shared Elena's philanthropic ideals.

The Minister wasn't a charismatic speaker. Lily watched people's attention wandering as he droned on. When he finished speaking and returned to his seat, Elena gave him a vulgar open-mouthed kiss that brought tremendous applause. Lily glanced at Carlos. Aside from a stern set to his expression, he gave no reaction to his ex-lover's performance.

Awards were handed out with speeches and Lily was mentally drifting off when she heard them call out Carlos's name. He patted her shoulder and then went up to speak at the microphone. The audience was attentive and laughed several times. He came back and slipped back into his chair resting his arm possessively around Lily's shoulders as he did so. Was that for show?

"Almost done," he whispered in her ear.

Juan Perez gave one more brief speech and then introduced the band. The dance floor was soon taken over by enthusiastic couples.

"Lily?" Carlos held out his hand to her.

"I haven't improved," she warned him.

"Trust me," was his response.

The other dancers hid them, so Lily relaxed. If she looked into his eyes it was easy enough to imagine they were alone. Carlos led her through several dances before her feet began to rebel against the new shoes. And she had another more pressing matter.

"Do you know where the washroom is?"

"Through those doors and turn left," he answered. "I will wait here."

Trying not to limp, she made her way to the washroom. It was a vision of lights, cut glass, and gilt frames in the outer room. The only thing lacking were gold toilets. They did have heated ceramic seats and automatic sensors. She'd love to hear her aunt's comments on this place.

After washing her hands, she sat down at one of the elaborate vanities to repair her make-up. Aside from a little smudging under her eyes, it had held up well. She dabbed a special paper on her face to blot the excess oil as she'd been instructed, re-pinned a curl that had escaped, and checked that her dress was still in the correct position.

"It is a pain, no?"

Lily turned, surprised to notice Elena had slipped into the vanity next to hers.

"Pardon me?"

"They make you to look just so to keep Carlos happy." Elena reapplied her blood red lipstick. "You have to watch that you don't drink too much, or laugh too loud. Heaven forbid you have your own mind."

Lily nodded politely and tried to think of a good exit line. The woman was obviously drunk.

"Well—"

"You are still new at this game. Naïve." Elena laughed with derision. "Carlos will get tired and throw you aside too, once you no longer suit his needs. I made the mistake of telling him I was with child. A glamorous mistress? *Si*. But to become fat and ugly to bear his child? He threw me out and destroyed my reputation. I loved him." She sniffed delicately and dabbed at the corners of her eyes with a tissue.

"I'm sorry—"

"Save the sorry. You will need it for yourself. He is charming now but you will see. One day you wake up and you are nothing to him. Mere chattel he has bought and no longer requires. Then you will experience his true nature. He is a violent man. Many women have the wounds to show for it. There are photographs." With a dignified huff, Elena stood to her full height and regally glided out of the powder room. Aside from her overcautious gait, Elena hid her inebriation well. Lily had seen the same attempt by her mother for several years until she had eventually stopped caring.

Lily remained at the vanity considering the woman's warning. Could she have fallen for another abusive man? Her stomach pitched in protest to the ugly thought. It wasn't possible. Carlos had been mean but he hadn't struck her. But what if Elena wasn't lying? Lily reapplied her lipstick and checked her teeth for any red telltale marks. With a shaky breath, she stood up to rejoin Carlos.

*

When Lily returned to the table, Carlos leaped up to meet her with a smile. Lily searched his enamored expression unwilling to believe he could do her physical harm.

"Ah *bella*, would you like another dance, or are you perhaps ready to leave?"

"Have you done all your business?"

"*Si*. It was important that I be here, but we need not stay."

"Oh good. My feet are killing me," she admitted. They said their farewells and headed for the door. Elena was making her way over to them but fortunately was stopped by an admiring fan. Lily didn't want to know what else the woman wished to say.

Chapter Twelve

Pale skin; long, curled eyelashes; and a fresh, unadorned smile. Carlos preferred Lily without all the make-up from the night before. But women did like to be pampered and he wanted to make her happy. He brushed a dark curl away from her eyes. She had held up beautifully at the business function. No one would've ever guessed she wasn't brought up among the socialite crowd in New York.

A slight frown crossed her features and he wondered what she was dreaming about. She seemed happy in Barcelona, exploring the countryside with her sketchbook in hand. He'd thought she would require more entertaining. Instead, he often had to persuade her to put down her sketchpad to go out.

Carlos reviewed his plans. Today he was taking her to the matinee performance of the Cavalia Equestrian Show and then tomorrow they flew back to New York. Carlos sighed. He could send her back by herself; she had even suggested that. But he didn't want to. She should stay in Barcelona, but unfortunately, he had promised to have her home in time for her class show. And he did have his meeting in New York on Wednesday.

Then there was the matter of the pre-nup. His lawyer had drawn it up, but Carlos hadn't decided how to present it. Surely she wouldn't expect him to marry her after such a short time, but he did want her to move here. She made him feel alive. *Si*, he had been sleepwalking through life until he met Lily.

Carlos smiled as her eyes fluttered open.

"*Buenos dias, mi amor.*" He kissed her forehead and gathered her closer. "Did you sleep well?"

"Yup." Lily purred.

Her eyelashes tickled against his chest. He stroked her hair away from her face. "I have a good idea. You should stay in Barcelona." He watched her expression carefully.

"Well, we do have another day before I have to be back in New York," Lily answered playfully, her hand moving suggestively down his chest.

"After your show opens, we could pack up your belongings for you to bring here." He kept his voice casual.

"What?" Her hand froze on his body.

"Or I could buy you everything new, but you don't seem to enjoy shopping."

"I don't need anything new—"

"Well that is simple, then. You can keep your apartment for visits, if you'd like. Or," Carlos pretended it was a new thought, "we could get a bigger one in Manhattan."

"What?" Lily suddenly sounded more awake. "You're thinking of moving to New York?"

"Not moving there," he corrected her. "My business is in Barcelona. But we could get a nice place in New York and visit often."

"Um, I live there."

"But you like it here?"

"It's lovely," she agreed. "But what about my school and work?"

"I could find you classes here. And you could focus full time on your art. Don't answer, just think about it." Carlos kissed her before she could protest more. She didn't seem enthusiastic but perhaps she was not good at accepting change. With time she would see he was right.

*

As they waited for some show to begin, Lily was still considering the possibilities. If she lived in Barcelona, could she do massages at

Carlos's mansion? That seemed very odd and there was the logistics of getting clients. But she couldn't just live off him. Maybe she could get a job in a spa in town. Would she need a work visa? Could she learn enough Spanish? Carlos had said his staff spoke English but if that was his idea of bilingual, then others might be the same. Oh God, it was too complicated.

The sound of hoof beats drew her attention to a man and a horse cantering onto the stage. The rider suddenly flung himself from the horse until he was dangling by his feet from the saddle, with his head and arms almost touching the ground. She let out a startled gasp.

"They are amazing, no?" Carlos asked with a smile.

"Yeah. Is this what you wanted to do?"

"*Si*. If a show like *Cavalia* had come through twelve years ago when I was still at the *Universidad*, I would not have finished. Look, here comes the man on two horses."

The rider was standing with a foot on each horse as they galloped into the ring. The horses ran under a bar and the rider deftly jumped over it and landed securely again on the horses as they continued running. More trick riders followed, each doing seemingly impossible feats of daring at high speed on horses. Several times, she covered her eyes with fear, opening them only at the burst of applause indicating the performers had survived.

Lily much preferred the dance segments that displayed the grace and beauty of the performers. Then there were people suspended from large ropes replicating many of the balletic movements of the horses and riders below them. The acts kept appearing one after the other until finally there was a crescendo in the music and the grand finale unfolded with breathtaking precision.

Lily was physically drained from just watching the performance.

"Do you still want to do that kind of riding?" she asked cautiously as they walked back to the car.

"No. I do not wish to break bones now that I am not twenty."
He shrugged. "Dreams are for the young and foolish."

"You're only thirty-two. You make it sound like you're eighty."

"I am not thirty-two. Where did you hear that?"

"I Googled you. You knew that. That's how I got your e-mail
address," she reminded him.

"Well, they lied. I am thirty-three. Almost eighty."

"When's your birthday?"

"Why?"

"So I can send you a cookie-gram. God! What's with the big
secrecy?" she huffed as he opened the car door for her.

"I don't have time for birthdays. That is for you young people."
He stood holding the door.

"I'm not getting in until you tell me your birthday." She folded
her arms over her chest.

"I could drive away."

"You wouldn't leave a poor girl stranded in a foreign country."
Lily batted her eyes at him playfully.

After a small pause Carlos said, "June 26. Now can we go?"

"Show me some ID."

"What?"

"You heard me. Prove it."

He flipped open his wallet and flashed his driver's license, then
quickly pocketed it again. Lily shook her head slowly and leaned
against the car with her hand out.

"You are a pain." He handed his wallet to her, watched her for
a moment and then held his hand out. "Satisfied?"

"Wait. I'm still trying to read this. *Febrero* 26, 1980. Hey! Your
birthday was yesterday."

"*Sí*, and you never sent me a cookie," he grumbled, retrieving
his wallet. "Now will you get in the car?"

"Okay." Lily waited until he'd started the engine. "Happy
belated birthday."

"*Gracias.* Now onto more important things, are you hungry?"

"Sure. You know I would've drawn a picture for you, or at least sung happy birthday."

"I got my own birthday present. You." Carlos leaned over and kissed her. "We will get an early dinner and then make some plans."

"Okay." Lily answered.

*

Sitting in the rustic café, Carlos studied Lily's expression as she read the pre-nup. She didn't look happy. Maybe she was concentrating on the legal language. He'd instructed his lawyer to write it as simply as possible, but much like asking doctors to write legibly, it seemed against their nature.

The settlements were incredibly generous. His lawyer had protested the amount of money he gave up if they broke up after less than one year, but he figured then she could at least afford a better apartment in New York.

"If you have any questions…" Carlos offered.

"Why?"

He shook his head in confusion. "This is fairly standard protection for both of us. If you move here, you will be taking a big chance leaving behind your life in New York. That is why if we break up, you get a minimum of a million dollars to restart your life wherever you choose."

"But you are planning how we will break up before we move in together." She looked hurt.

"No. As I said this is standard procedure. I am not planning for us to separate." Carlos tried to contain his impatience. "It would be foolhardy to assume that it could not happen. We have to be realistic."

"Oh." Lily resumed reading the document. Her nose crinkled in distaste and he tried to figure out what part she was on. She reached the end of the document. She carefully folded it several times and then put it in her purse. Finally she raised her eyes to his.

"I will read this over again and let you know."

"You can suggest other things in there if you'd like." Carlos wondered again if there was a language problem.

The waiter stopped by their table.

"*¿Querriás mas café?*"

"No, *gracias*." Carlos turned to Lily as he paid the bill. "Shall we go back to the house so you can finish your painting?"

"Yes, that'd be nice."

The car ride back to the house was uncomfortable. Even the marvelous architecture failed to elicit a response from her. When they arrived, Lily got her watercolors and disappeared out back. No further discussion seemed possible.

As it got darker, Carlos felt a building sense of unease. What the hell was wrong with her? Surely she couldn't have expected more money. Or did she want a marriage proposal? Certainly not that quickly. Maybe she didn't understand the contract.

He went in search of Lily and found her immersed in her painting down by the beach.

"That is beautiful." He spoke quietly so as not to startle her.

"Thank you. I'm almost finished." She continued in silence for a while more. "Okay. I'm done." She smiled up at him before packing away her paints.

"*Bueno*. Federico is making us churros and hot chocolate."

She took his hand as they climbed back up to the house. Maybe she had come around. He pulled her close for a kiss and after a brief hesitation; she kissed him back with her usual enthusiasm. A great weight lifted off his chest.

"*Mi amor*," he murmured, his hand lightly tracing the edge of her hairline. "You are so beautiful, like a fawn at daybreak." He kissed her forehead before they continued up the path.

*

The churros were delicious, but the conversation was strained. Lily tried desperately not to think about the document stashed in her purse. It felt like she had to decide her whole life in one day. And yet she didn't have enough information. She didn't really believe his ex-fiancée that Carlos was violent. Still, she couldn't just ignore the warning. And often the first move of abusive men was to isolate the prey from their families. A foreign country and a different language were as isolating as you could get.

And the money in the pre-nup was way too much—which brought her back to Elena's prophetic words. "Women are merely things to be bought, used and discarded like garbage."

Still, rich men often had contracts to guard against gold-diggers, so maybe she was over-reacting. Alimonies and palimonies were astronomical these days. The personal conduct clauses seemed odd, as if specifically tailored to control her behavior. It also felt like a one-sided purchase of her sexual favors. Did he still consider her a high-priced prostitute? God, she was going to strain her brain from so much back and forthing.

And at the back of her mind, she couldn't help but acknowledge that a million dollars meant she'd never have to struggle to pay rent again. But she'd survived this far without selling herself and she wasn't prepared to give up her morals now. And she couldn't risk getting involved with an abusive man again. It had been a marvelous dream that someone like Carlos could actually love her. Unfortunately, reality had a terrible habit of waking you up. Whether he was abusive or just paying for her sexual favors, neither were acceptable choices.

Earlier she had mused briefly on what he would say if she had Aunt Lilith write up a counter contract. *The party of the first part, Carlos, is hereby required to shtup the party of the second part daily and then to leave her alone so she can do more important things. The first party will receive escalating bonuses for his stud services for as long as he can satisfactorily provide them.* Lily wished her aunt were here to help sort through all this crap.

After dessert when they strolled through the rolling countryside, Carlos acted as if nothing had changed between them. He kept stopping to point out interesting views and to kiss her. The views became less frequent and the kisses more. Each kiss lasted a little longer and more searing than the previous until Lily wondered if they would make it back to the mansion with their clothes intact.

Funny that as soon as she contemplated the bleakness of leaving Carlos, her body was desperate for him. Well if their fling was ending, then she should at least have fun on her way out.

She walked sedately up the stairs ahead of him feeling the intensity of his focus behind her. Did he somehow know that she was planning to leave? Perhaps that was his goal all along. She didn't like to think he was that devious, but then again, it was no better if he thought her a prostitute. She determinedly shut off her brain. She would not let anything destroy tonight.

Carlos closed the bedroom door behind them and she turned to face him. With a slow seductive smile, she slid her t-shirt over her head. His eyes swept to the lacy bra barely concealing her breasts. He seemed frozen in place as he stared, mesmerized. Lily wiggled her hips, dragging the jeans down with deliberation. How far could she push it before she felt ridiculous? He seemed to be hanging on her every move. She peeled off her jeans and socks and then bent at the waist leaving her butt hanging in the air. The small lacy panties also apparently held great fascination for him as his Adam apple bobbed in response.

Lily licked her lips and slid her thumbs along the waistband of her underwear. Then she strolled toward him swaying her hips. Carlos reached for her but she batted his hands away. After removing his shirt and jeans, she slowly circled his body rubbing up against him in the process. Carlos's entire body tensed in anticipation.

Holding his hands at his sides, she stretched up to kiss him. His erection rubbed against her belly. She brought one of his hands to her breast and then curled her leg around his thigh. Carlos grabbed her butt and pulled her even closer. With a low moan, he lifted her other leg around his thigh and walked over to lay her on the bed.

His lips and tongue played gently on her breast teasing her through the flimsy cloth. Then he nibbled his way slowly to her mouth. Lily looked at his intense brown eyes as he kissed her. It felt like he loved her, but maybe that was just the look of a man in lust. What did she know? She threw her head back and closed her eyes when he nuzzled at her neck.

"Mmm," she murmured, directing his hand between her legs. Her own hand closed on his erection. "You feel so good." He was hard and yet the skin was silky soft. Lily wanted to physically memorize every part of his body. And it seemed everything she did turned him on even more.

"Ah, Lily." His breath was ragged. "I need you."

He slid her panties down her body and then kissed where they had been. She gasped at the swirling sensation building inside her. Her hips bucked to the pounding rhythm he created, wanting more, needing more until suddenly her world exploded.

"Oh God, Carlos, I love you!" she cried out as her body crumbled into a thousand pieces. She gasped to regain her breath, collapsing back onto the bed. He kissed his way up her body. His gentle caresses calmed her shuddering nerves. Dear Lord, had she said that out loud? Maybe, she hoped, she prayed, she had just thought it.

Carlos kissed her mouth gently and then shifted his lips to her ear.

"*Mi angelita.*"

Lily reached for a condom and covered him. He eased in slowly, filling her and then more. It was heavenly. She took his nipple in her teeth suckling him as he rocked within her. His breath caught again, empowering her as she bit gently up his neck. Their bodies careened together, needing the violence and the speed. She fought for her breath as he continued to bring her to the brink and then slide away. With a gasp she flew over the edge again, crying out as her senses all centered on the raging climax within her. Carlos let out a guttural cry in response and they clung to each other as if their lives depended on it.

How can this not be love? She had never shared so passionately or been made to feel so special. Could a man have sex like this and still not love the woman he was with?

Lily knew the answer before she'd even finished formulating the question. Yes. Men were hard wired differently. The psych class she had audited at NYU had spent a great deal of time on the differences between male and female brains. If he didn't say, "I love you," don't assume it. But what she would give to hear those precious words. She inched in closer to his warm body hoping against hope. His arm pulled her closer still, but *"mi angelita,"* was his sole utterance.

Chapter Thirteen

Lily checked all the drawers for her black sweater. Maria had taken it away to be washed and it hadn't come back. The pants and underwear had reappeared, so she wore those with her new t-shirt and hoodie and hoped she would be warm enough in New York. Still, it gave her a good excuse to seek out the housekeeper.

Maria was in the drawing room dusting in between the vases and statues.

"Escusee." Lily hoped that was a word. "Maria?"

"*Si*, Li-lee."

"Do you know where my black sweater is?"

"*Que?*" The woman smiled vaguely.

"Sweater," Lily pointed at her white shirt. "*Negro?*"

"No," Maria shook her head. "Blanco."

Damn. *Try something else.* "Question. *Esta* Carlos ever… *violentado?*" That didn't even sound right to Lily.

Maria looked blank so Lily pretended to be boxing someone. "Carlos?"

Maria brightened with comprehension. "*A si el caso con los toros fue mui violente.*"

"But Carlos." What else had Elena said? Oh yeah. "*Las photographias de Carlos violente?*" She again mimed a fighter.

"Ah, si, Malo." Maria pretended to punch herself in the face and then lay down on the floor. "Ughhh!"

Lily's stomach plummeted. Maybe she was talking about something else. "Carlos?" She punched one more time.

Maria stood and nodded. "*Si.*"

"Oh." Lily stood there wondering what else to say. "Um, well. I go now—*vamanos. Buenos dias. Gracias.*" She hugged the woman and turned away.

*

Lily grabbed her purse and the sketchbook she'd already started on and was ready to go. Everything felt surreal, as if there were two opposing realities occurring at the same time. Her body remembered Carlos's thrilling lovemaking last night and the way he'd lavished her with attention, while her brain tried to reconcile the image of him as a violent abuser. It didn't seem possible. And yet some of the conduct clauses in the pre-nup could be there to protect his image if he hit her.

Carlos was putting his computer bag into the car. Lily watched him for a moment, admiring his graceful movements. He was too handsome and cultured for someone like her. When he turned and saw her, his smile transformed his features from the impatient businessman to the contented lover in a second.

"*Hola, mi amor*. You are ready to go?"

"I guess so."

They slid into the back of the car and Lily naturally fit into Carlos's embrace. How could something wrong feel so right? But it was. To be fooled once was forgivable, but she couldn't let herself be lulled into a second abusive relationship. Lily glanced out the window.

This fling had been good for her. She had discovered new places, new confidence in herself as a woman, and a stronger sense of who she was. Unfortunately, that person wasn't someone who could let herself be bought even by someone as tempting as Carlos. She let out an involuntary sigh.

"What is it, *mi angelita?*"

"Nothing. It is so beautiful here."

"I am glad you love it as much as I. So why did you not use the clay or oils? Were they not a good quality?"

"No. I'm sure it was fine. Watercolors are much faster so I knew I could finish them in a couple of days. I didn't want to leave a half-finished mess."

"That would be acceptable. The kiln will arrive later this week."

Lily felt guilty not telling him of her plans. But it was better to get home first. Not that she worried about how he'd take it—from the speed with which he'd produced the legal paper, he'd probably presented it to several other lovers along the way—but she didn't want to spend a seven-hour flight defending her decision. He'd said he had more business in New York, so it wasn't like she was dragging him out on false pretenses. And she had offered to fly back commercial by herself.

*

Even on the plane, Carlos could not draw Lily out of her quiet mood. Was she worried about leaving her home in New York? It was a big step. Still she was moving into a life with no worries or responsibilities. Surely that must be comforting. And Lily moving to Barcelona was the only logical way for them to be together. Obviously, that was what they both wanted.

Last night had been incredible. Lily had surprised him yet again with her luscious seduction. She had grown so much from the uncertain girl crying after making love to a woman secure enough to take what she wanted. And to give completely of herself. They had made love well into the morning until he hadn't been sure his body could continue but somehow…Carlos smiled remembering the last exhausted embrace as they'd finally drifted off to sleep.

He put his arm around her and kissed her head. Lily was sketching again but this time it seemed to be abstract forms.

"What is this?"

"I'm just doodling to figure the form of a new sculpture. Sometimes it helps to visualize it on paper first."

"Ah." A sudden surge of loneliness surprised him when she turned back to her drawing. He had never felt emotionally dependent on anyone before. *Muy complicado.*

With a frown, Carlos opened his computer to work out his strategy for the business meeting on Wednesday. The communications he'd received from the Americans had been promising. If he played his cards right, the merger should be well under way by next year. His hand poised above the keyboard, Carlos was distracted by the woman beside him. Something felt amiss, but how could it be? He absently stroked her shoulder while staring at his laptop. Lily put down her book and snuggled into his embrace.

"I'm going to nap, if that's okay?" Lily asked as she rested her head on his chest.

"Of course." Carlos put his computer away and reclined back with her.

"You can keep working."

"After you kept me up all night, I cannot," Carlos answered with a smile. He sensed her blush without looking. How the demanding seductress of last night could change into the sweet innocent by day was an endless wonder. When he thought back to his first impression of her as a young ruffian, and then the image of the angry woman splattered in clay, he realized he was still learning more about her daily.

*

Several hours, a movie, snacks and more doodling passed before they finally landed. Lily wondered how she was going to let Carlos know of her decision. He would be upset if for no other reason than he was used to getting his own way. Was it merely wishful thinking or did he really did care for her? The sex was fabulous, but he probably had marvelous sex with every lover. And if he found himself another model type, he wouldn't have to spend so much money and time trying to get them to look and act right.

She sighed as she gathered up her meager belongings. She'd taken two new shirts and a sketchpad but lost her black sweater.

Not too bad a deal. She'd lost a lot more to Danny when she'd fled that relationship. And she hadn't gained anything. Carlos broke into her thoughts.

"There is the car." Carlos slipped his arm around her waist and led her along the rain-slicked tarmac. He gave her address to the driver as he helped into the back seat. Lily sat back and snuggled into his embrace. It was going to make it more difficult when they had to part, but it felt so good. Carlos kissed the top of her head and she fought back her tears.

After a long silent drive, they arrived outside her apartment.

"Pick up anything from your apartment you'll need for tonight. We will come back tomorrow to gather what you'll want in Barcelona." Carlos opened the car door for her, oblivious to her discomfort.

"I'm not going back to Barcelona." Lily looked at his confused expression. She reached into her purse, pulled out the folded paper and handed it to him.

"I cannot sign this. I'm not for sale. Thank you for everything." She pressed her lips together, determined not to cry.

"What do you mean?" He looked more shocked than she expected.

"I can't be who you want me to be. I'm sorry. I do care for you, but it is not enough."

"What is not enough? You want more money?" Carlos was imposing, almost scary, in his anger.

"How dare you say that? I don't want your stupid money." *God, Elena was right. He thought of her as an expensive, but disposable plaything. The cheap American tart he picked up in the Dominican Republic.*

"Perhaps we have not found your price yet." His eyes blazed.

Lily's hand connected with his face before she even realized what she was doing. Only when she heard the loud smack and felt the sting on the palm of her hand did she fully take in her actions. With a gasp, she swung around and ran to the door of her apartment.

As she struggled to fit the key into the lock, she heard Carlos's car swiftly pull away. How had she allowed herself to be fooled twice by the same man? And yet, when things were going well between them he seemed to honestly care for her. If she could only have ignored Elena's warning or if he hadn't rushed her with that contract. She'd been so happy with him. He made her feel beautiful, inside and out.

Lily unlocked the door to her building with a sense of dread. Everything was bleak, gray and cold. She hadn't known him that long, but life without Carlos seemed unfathomable. No more gentle teasing. No more passionate love. Never to walk with his arm comfortably holding her close.

By the time she had gotten to her apartment door, her cheeks were wet with tears. Should she call him and apologize? No. The steely look of anger when she refused his contract flashed in her mind. She couldn't risk him turning violent. She couldn't understand Maria's complacent attitude to her boss' anger but the woman laid flat out on the floor had left Lily no room for doubt. The second lock stuck and she hit the door in frustration. Everything in her life had turned against her.

Finally inside, she didn't feel any better. The room was confining and the stale air held the conflicting odors of her neighbors' cooking and cigar smoke from the man downstairs. She threw out the orchids Carlos had brought her and her tears started gushing all over again. Damn. With a box of tissues, she crawled under the blankets on her couch and tried to turn off her brain.

*

Carlos paced his hotel room in frustration. *Dios*, what was wrong with that woman? Was it a ploy to get more money or make him propose marriage? And yet she hadn't even appeared to be expecting him to fight with her; she had seemed more resigned. When had she decided? Surely not last night when they had that phenomenal sex. She had screamed that she loved him and then the next day rejected him.

The phone rang and Carlos snatched it up, hoping it was Lily.

"*Si.*" Carlos listened impatiently. "I will be there tomorrow at eleven. *Gracias.*" He hung up abruptly. It was good his meeting was moved up a day. He could finish his business and get home. New York held no appeal for him. He would complete the deal and leave all this behind.

Chapter Fourteen

Anna peered critically at Lily. "Every time you quit this man you lose more weight. You are too thin."

"Well, that's it then, I won't break up with him again," Lily joked. "Just think, if we could market this break-up thing, we could have the next big diet craze."

"But I don't understand why you leave him; he was rich and took you to nice places."

Lily studied the black dirt embedded under her short nails. Even with the leather gloves, welding made your hands look disgusting. Oh well, who cared what her hands looked like anyway? "Let's just say I learned something about him I couldn't deal with."

Anna's eyes widened with excitement. "Is he into weird sex practices? Did he want you to spank him?"

"Ewww, no."

"What? Swinging? Bondage? Menage—"

"No. Stop. It's nothing like that." Lily sighed. It figured with Anna's poor language skills, those would be the few terms she knew. "His ex-girlfriend told me he had beaten other women."

"His ex-girlfriend? Maybe she lied."

"I wondered, so I asked his housekeeper."

"And she confirmed it?"

"Well, she didn't speak English, but she implied there were photographs of Carlos knocking someone out."

"Did you ask him?"

"No. Of course he'd deny being abusive. And then he wanted me to move to Barcelona. He handed me this four-page document to sign outlining how much money I'd get when we broke up and all the things I couldn't do."

"A prenuptial contract? It is not unusual."

"It's not like he asked me to marry him. He just wanted to rent my services. Who pays someone a million bucks to be their girlfriend? The contract was to make sure I didn't embarrass him. And the money aspect was laid out so I got more 'bonuses' the longer I stayed or kept him interested."

Anna looked at her in confusion. "Could be for your protection, no?"

"That's what he said, but it was so one-sided. I sleep with him, I get rich. He sleeps with me, he gets nothing. So who's selling what? Plus I had to agree not to pose nude or sell stories about him or our relationship to any magazines."

"You want to pose nude?" Anna asked in surprise.

"No. But why would he put something like that in unless he was worried I'd tell someone he beat me?" This conversation was not going right. It had been so clear before.

Anna smiled. "Magazines pay big bucks for dirt on celebrities."

"Anyway, it doesn't matter why or what happened. Carlos and I are no longer seeing each other. *Finito,* as he would say." Lily frowned. "Or is that Italian? I'm confused."

"Maybe you should think about this a little more. I mean, if you know he's abusive that's one thing, but to just go on other people's word…" She shrugged. "Unless he's a lousy lover; then you break up."

"No. It wasn't that." Lily sighed. She wished she could forget how good he made her feel.

"You could be his part time lover. Then if he hit you, you leave."

"No, I'm not good at casual. Even knowing it was a fling with Carlos, I got way too attached." Lily scrunched her eyes to keep from crying. She'd done way too much of that already.

"A friend tell me," Anna's eyes lit up with humor as she tried to recall the line, "'A hard man is good to find. And a rich one, even better.'"

"I'll keep that in mind." Lily hugged her friend. "I have to go. I've got a client in forty minutes and I have to clean up. Thanks for the coffee."

*

"I got the red dot!" Lily shouted to a classmate as she passed him in the hallway.

"Congratulations. I haven't seen the show yet, but I'll check it out at lunch," he replied.

Lily hoped she'd see someone else she could tell. Anna had disappeared again and a few others seemed to have left for March break. *Darn.* She had gotten the blue dot a few times in previous class shows, which was an honorable mention. This was her first red dot, which meant the school wanted to buy her piece for their collection.

She phoned Lilith, who was excited for her, but she really wanted to tell Carlos. Despite saying nice things about her paintings, he'd seemed to think her art was more a hobby than a career. It didn't matter. He was out of her life now. It was difficult to believe only two weeks had passed since she'd last seen him. It felt like ages except that the pain was still so raw.

Lily went back to the basement to work on her current sculpture. It was an abstract of a woman reaching up and letting go. The lines were beautiful, but somehow the releasing felt like pulling back. Was that in the sculpture or just her emotions? Lily continued to refine the piece wondering if sculpture could be a form of psychotherapy, perhaps a two-dimensional Rorschach test.

It could be her subconscious was saying she should swallow her pride and call Carlos. She had been miserable without him. He'd probably already found her replacement, someone more suitable. Lily realized with a jolt she didn't even have a phone number for him, only an e-mail address.

Would she go back to him if he asked her? That question reverberated in her brain. She should continue studying and become a real artist. If she were secure in her own career, she wouldn't have to worry about being considered arm-candy or a mere sexual plaything. And then maybe she'd meet someone who'd treat her as an equal. She sighed. She'd never meet anyone as amazing as Carlos again. Someone like him came along only once in a lifetime, if that.

*

Nursing a Scotch at a small bar overlooking *Avenida Litoral,* Carlos made notes on the amended merger agreement that his colleague from Anderson Cordell had faxed him earlier. Carlos had driven a hard bargain and the Americans had given in to every one of his demands. He nodded as the bartender placed a bowl of spiced corn nuts before him.

If he'd planned on dicing and selling the company, then his negotiations would've been fine. Since he wanted the merged companies to function as a cohesive team, he'd gone too far. His anger at Lily's rejection had flavored his business judgment and now he had to return to New York to soften the terms. Not something he enjoyed, but it would engender goodwill toward Stella Sociedad and ultimately make his life easier.

He scanned his itinerary for the New York meeting. He didn't notice the seat beside him had filled up until the waft of expensive perfume invaded his nostrils. As always, she knew exactly when she had his attention.

"You've lost your little American, Carlos. What a shame. Did she wise up to your cruel nature, or did you give her the boot, too?"

"*Hola,* Elena," Carlos acknowledged and then turned away.

"No it can't be! She rejected you? I didn't think she had it in her. She seemed so meek when we had our little heart to heart."

"What are you talking about?" He turned to stare at her, careful not to sound too interested.

"Hm? Oh, nothing." Elena paused. When he remained silent she continued, "We had a long chat at the awards dinner. She was so sympathetic about you deserting our baby."

"It is not my baby, as you know," he corrected her warily.

"I always felt your disapproval. I drank too much. I attracted too much attention. No woman can please you, Carlos." Elena stood up onto her mile-high heels. "And she had not heard about you beating up women."

Carlos inhaled sharply. "I never hit you or any other woman."

"Then why did she believe me?" Without a backwards glance, she carefully walked back to a table where the Minister of Trade was seated, eyeing Carlos suspiciously.

Carlos tossed back the rest of his drink and left the bar. Could Lily have believed Elena and not him? It did not make sense.

*

The grinding of the landing gear unfolding brought Carlos out of his daydream. He was usually more productive when traveling. He flipped through his mail. The usual pleas for donations to various charities. Yes. No. No. Yes. Several proposals for new business deals. He fastened his seatbelt and put away his papers.

At least he no longer had to bother about the tabloids. At first the papers had been thrilled to report the name of his new *amante,* along with her picture at the awards night. They soon lost interest when she was no longer shrouded in mystery. *El Primo* had recalled its New York spy. He suspected Elena had alerted the reporters about his trip to the Dominican Republic to deflect criticism of her own indiscretion. She certainly knew most of the paparazzi by name. Had Elena really told Lily he had hit her? Or was she lying now?

Perhaps it was fate that he was back in New York. Not that he usually gave much credence to powers outside of his control, but he could use this trip to find out the reason for Lily's rejection.

Looking out at the sunny view of Manhattan from his limo, Carlos felt lighter than he had for days. Even the weather was more amenable. New York was usually raining on his visits. Sunshine transformed the gray dullness into a vista of tall buildings with brightly glinting windows punctuated by trees bursting out in fresh buds.

Carlos shifted his attention back to work and completed his agenda for the merger meeting. Now he was free to enjoy the last few miles of his trip to the hotel. As they stopped at a light, he noticed his driver waving dismissively. He glanced out the window at a squeegee man dressed in gray rags doggedly smearing the windows with a filthy cloth. His driver appeared ready to take on the old guy. Carlos opened his window.

"*Aquí*." He held out a handful of bills to the surprise of both his driver and the bum.

The guy scooped the money and hastily wiped the viscous slime off the window before the light changed.

"You only encourage them more," his driver remarked grumpily.

"Those people have to eat."

"That's the job of the government, not me." With that, the driver rolled up the privacy window.

Carlos wondered if he'd hit a sore spot with his driver. It was no concern of his. They pulled up to the hotel and Carlos checked his watch. He still had half an hour to relax before he had to suit up for the meeting. A shower, change his shirt, and he would be ready. He wasn't sure why he felt good today but it could only bode well.

*

The meeting had been productive. There was still a lot of work to be done, but the first hurdle of the merger had been cleared. He had a consultation in three days with the chief financial officer and then another one later on with human resources. This time he would not leave New York until he was satisfied they were on the right track.

Carlos celebrated with a stroll through Central Park. The warming weather had brought out tourists and native New Yorkers alike and the park teemed with goodwill. A winding path deposited him on Sixtieth Street, and on a whim, he decided to check out Lily's art school. He was pretty sure it was somewhere nearby from his previous research.

He probably wouldn't have noticed the building except for the handful of oddly dressed students smoking outside on the steps. Bandanas, ripped denim and multiple t-shirts were worn by the majority, but a couple of the older women were sporting paint-smeared smocks and sneakers. Carlos smiled and walked into the building. A man sitting at a podium just inside the door watched silently as Carlos walked towards the elevator.

"Excuse me, sir." An older woman with a tight black bun and a rumpled blue blouse ran out of the office to stop him. "Are you here to meet someone or...?" Her face radiated suspicion.

"I saw in your window there is a sculpture exhibit," Carlos answered.

"Yes. On the third floor. But you have to sign in before you can go up." She glared at the guard and directed Carlos back to the office. "And I'll need some photo ID."

"All right." Carlos watched amused as she took his driver's license and checked the photo against his face. She gave his ID to a young woman behind the counter, who deposited it in a plastic lock box and gave him a battered, laminated yellow paper.

Carlos signed the guest book, vaguely aware of whispering and giggling from a small group of girls behind him. He felt strangely out of place as he took the rickety elevator to the third floor. He was relieved to find the gallery fairly empty other than the art works.

The sculptures varied greatly in styles and skill levels. Would he be able to guess which was Lily's work? The first statue was a clean torso, the accompanying card stating unimaginatively, "Torso, by JoAnn Leeson, three hundred dollars." He was relieved it wasn't Lily's as it lacked her spark of imagination. The next two were better, but still without substance.

Carlos's eyes fell on the middle sculpture. It was of two figures, the female clutching onto the male who was reaching away for something or someone else. He couldn't look away. He walked around the sculpture several times, mesmerized by the lines of the figures in constant conflict. With growing discomfort, he read the accompanying card, "Casual Lie number thirty-two, by Lily Scott."

She was a talented artist. Her paintings had been pretty, but the emotions she evoked with her sculpture were phenomenal. The statue made him feel both guilt and sorrow for the sense of longing in the female figure's body language.

How had he thought of her as merely a dilettante at art? Still, she'd never sounded all that confident in her own work. And New York was filled with artist/waiters of dubious talent. Carlos found one other piece by Lily, a sweet alabaster sculpture of a musical note wrapped seductively around a treble clef. They seemed to be caught in a tango. He admired her first piece again and then left the gallery quickly.

Carlos strode back downtown trying to order his thoughts. Perhaps she had felt he didn't take her seriously as an artist. He had bought her art supplies, but hadn't taken into account that she might wish a fulfilling career as well.

He needed to find out more about Lily Scott. A personal merger was much more important than a business one and yet clearly he hadn't done due diligence on the woman. This investigation he would do himself.

*

Two hours later, riding the elevator up to Ms. Lilith Scott's apartment, Carlos straightened his tie and shot his cuffs. It was difficult to know what sort of reception to expect. The woman had recognized his name instantly when he called, which probably was not a good sign. The apartment door swung open as he exited the elevator.

"Mr. Diego? We finally meet." The woman gave him a stern once over from head to toe. "I'm Lily's Aunt Lilith. To what do I owe the pleasure of your company?"

Her blue eyes were vividly expressive much like Lily's, but the similarity between the two women stopped there. Lily often seemed to be dressing to hide in a crowd, whereas this woman's attire of bright colors screamed for attention. From the neon stripes in her peasant skirt to the many-layered contrasting blouses, she was visually arresting. Even her curly hair was an interesting mixture of red hues not found in nature. When she ushered him into her apartment his eyes were drawn to the colorfully decorated cast on her right arm. Even that made a fashion statement.

"First, I apologize for your unfortunate accident at the art showing." Carlos indicated the cast.

"How did you—?" Lilith's eye's narrowed suspiciously. "Are you not the man who met my niece on vacation?"

"Yes. I am also the owner of Stella Sociadad. My company sponsored the Klimt show at which…" He sensed her anger building as she pieced together his total involvement.

"You sent me that ticket to the Dominican Republic." Her face tightened with comprehension and her voice rose in pitch. "And you seduced poor Lily thinking she was me to forestall a lawsuit, you conniving bugger!"

"No. It was not like that." Carlos backed up in case she took a swing at him. "I was unaware who Lily was at first, then when I believed she was suing my company, I—" Carlos stopped. How much had Lily told this woman about him?

"You called her a cheap whore and demoralized the poor girl." Lilith finished for him.

"I more than apologized for my atrocious behavior." He would not be browbeaten by this woman any longer. "Surely she can't still be blaming me for that."

"That would seem to be just the tip of the iceberg." Lilith considered him, her lips pursed with tension. "So why are you here? Did Lily prick your poor macho ego?"

"I had hoped you could explain Lily's actions." He let out a terse sigh. "It is obvious I should not have come." With a slight bow, Carlos turned to leave.

"Cut the bullshit." She fixed him with an antagonistic glare. "Lily's already been through hell. The last thing she needs is another asshole using her as a punching bag."

"She claims I hit her?" He shook his head, stunned.

"No. But she's sensible enough to run from someone with a history of abuse," Lilith shot back.

"I have never hit a woman." Carlos strode back toward the elevator before adding, "Check your sources before you slander a man."

"But your housekeeper said…"

"Maria?" Carlos snorted in disbelief. "She would not say such a thing, nor would she work for me if she believed that. You are mistaken."

She persisted. "Lily said there were photos."

He punched the call button for the elevator. He'd have preferred to put his fist through the wall. He kept his voice calm. "The gossip magazines dug up some old police photographs of Lily with bruises and cuts and claimed it was my doing."

"Photos of Lily?"

"*Si. El Primo* had a journalist, Anna Gomez, at the art school collecting information."

"Lily's friend, Anna? Oh shit!" Lilith took a couple of steps into the hallway, her eyes still narrowed with suspicion. "Then why did you offer her so much money? She thought it was to protect your reputation."

"My ex-fiancée is suing for much more and she is already wealthy. I wanted Lily to feel secure."

"You scared the living shit out of her." Lilith laughed and then started coughing.

"Are you all right?" Carlos asked. Should he should pat her back, or would she slug him?

She held up her hand. "Give me a sec." Her face was red as she got her hacking under control. "If what you say is true, I'm sorry. But even so, Lily is not one of your celebrity women to be played with and then thrown aside. She needs a nice, simple boy who will love her the way she is."

"I do love her," he interrupted. The proclamation seemed to surprise him more than Lilith. *But it was true. Why hadn't he seen it before?*

"Did you ever tell her?"

"*Dios,* no." The elevator finally opened. "I must go. Please do not tell Lily you have seen me." Carlos stepped into the lift. "And thank you for your candor."

Chapter Fifteen

Carlos slipped surreptitiously through the turnstile and down the grungy, ammonia-scented stairs of the subway station. He wondered again about his sanity. How had he come to this? Wearing jeans, a dark hoodie, and running shoes, he looked nothing like the successful businessman of the previous week. He'd even traded in his laptop case for one of the ubiquitous backpacks he saw everywhere. And he had become more invisible as he quickly learned the ins and outs of underground travel.

At first, he had been faintly alarmed at the chaotic hustling and pushiness of the swirling mass of humanity. Following Lily without her noticing had proved extremely challenging until he relaxed into his newfound role of private investigator. He could've asked Lily's aunt to help him win her back, but in a way this felt more like he was actually discovering the real Lily. He'd judged her too many times without actually understanding her. And with this knowledge, he would find a way to win her back.

Carlos hadn't listened to her concerns in Barcelona. He'd assumed she would fit into his life with him purchasing whatever she missed in New York. No wonder she'd felt like he was buying her. What could he possibly say or do now to make amends?

A large woman pushed past Carlos into the subway car dragging a sullen child behind her. Sticky chocolate fingers left a smear on his jeans that he decided to ignore. The woman also pretended not to notice as she hustled the child further into the car. This week he'd found a different side of the city than he'd seen in all his previous visits. But he had developed a grudging admiration for the people maneuvering through the vast network of underground trains. It was incredible watching the crowds converge, disperse and then regroup as they filed from one train line to the next.

Carlos was also astounded at how much he enjoyed New York from this new perspective. He'd bought a hot pretzel from a cart on the street and walked around with a cup of coffee in a paper cup. It was a freedom he hadn't felt since he'd been a university student all those years ago. When had he become so set in his way?

And Lily never ceased to amaze him. She had projected a sweet and almost fragile persona when he'd met her in the Dominican Republic. Now he could see her incredible strength and purpose as she set about her daily routines.

After only a week, Carlos was seeing the patterns in her schedule. She was in school most mornings from nine to one. Monday, Tuesday, and Thursday afternoons she did massages at a downtown office and then she went to a studio to work in the evenings. Wednesdays she went back to school in the afternoon, and Fridays she went to her aunt's in the morning and then school in the afternoon. She hadn't been exaggerating when she'd said she had no time for a social life.

Carlos exited the train at Fifty-third and Fifth, checking first to see if Lily had noticed him when the crowd thinned out. Fortunately, she was engrossed in a book, oblivious to the outside world. His jaw set firmly, Carlos forced his way between a group of dawdling tourists.

"Excuse me." One of the ladies tapped him on the shoulder. "Do you know how we get to Penn Station?"

"*Sí*. Take the E train downtown and it will take you right there." Carlos smiled as he realized how much better he knew New York after only a week underground. Lily had been right about him not taking the time previously to enjoy life. Now, in his effort to win her back, he was learning not to take everything so much for granted. Work was important, but certainly not the only thing.

Carlos whistled tunelessly as he walked up to street level. It was time to get back to his hotel room, spruce up, and then tonight he would put his plans into action. He had spent much of his week trying to think how he could prove his love to her. It seemed *loco*, but at least she would know he was sincere.

*

Maybe she was going crazy? Lily thought she saw Carlos walking up from Fifty-fourth Street. And last week at school when she was walking down the stairs to the basement, she could've sworn she saw him getting out of the elevator. She ran out to the main hallway but he wasn't there. Was she hallucinating? Maybe Aunt Lilith was right, she should watch her diet.

It was silly to even think he would be at her school. He'd never expressed more than a passing interest in seeing her work. But then she'd never asked to see his office, and she hadn't oohed and aahed over his expensive toys either.

She kept thinking as the days went by she'd miss him less. After all, she'd gotten over him before. Well, almost. But somehow it was like a huge chunk of her life was missing, as though he'd always been there and now his absence left a gaping hole.

The police horses made her think of Carlos affectionately rubbing the nose of his horse in the Dominican Republic. The well-dressed mannequins in the men's stores made her remember the soft feel of his silky shirts. A whiff of a men's cologne with hints of sandalwood and vanilla would bring all sorts of sensual memories flooding into her brain. A deep warm voice, with or even without the Spanish accent, would cause her to turn her head hopefully.

And her life seemed somehow less fulfilling. Even the news that someone had bought her smaller sculpture from the show failed to excite her. She wanted Carlos to share her victories. But she had been the one to call it off so she couldn't complain now that she missed him. Lily finished her sculpting for the day and headed for her locker to clean up before going home.

"Hey, Scott! You going to the pub tonight?" A classmate was changing his pants at his locker. It was amazing how many of the guys at school were borderline exhibitionists.

"Nah. Maybe next week." Lily buried her head in her locker so she wouldn't have to see his skinny white legs. It was different with models because you were supposed to look at them.

"What? You're passing up on Kennedy's chocolate pecan pie? Won't you get the DTs if you quit cold turkey like that?"

"I'll take my chances. But have an extra slice for me. It'll help sop up all that beer you guys swig."

Lily was amazed at how much more friendly people had become since she'd met Carlos. Or had she become more open to others? She didn't feel so much of an outsider.

She took off her bandana and fluffed out her hair. It looked stupid but the bandana did keep all the stone dust from sticking in her hair. Supposedly the stone dust could make you go bald if you weren't careful. That would be embarrassing.

A short walk to Fifty-third and Seventh, the E train to Twenty-third Street, and change to the G train to Greenpoint Station. The cool sunny weather was a pleasant surprise. There was just enough wind to clear out the urine smells in the stairways and the panhandlers seemed mellower as well. She gave one guy a bit of change and got a card depicting the alphabet in American Sign Language in return. She amused herself by practicing the letters on the way home.

A beep on her cell phone indicated a new message just as Lily came in her door. She flipped it open to listen.

"Hi sweetie. It's me. Could you meet me at seven at the Zodiak Club on Eighth Avenue at Forty-fourth? I have some exciting news. See you later."

Aunt Lilith at a club on Eighth Avenue? That didn't seem right. Lily called her aunt back immediately, but got her machine and had to leave a message. Damn. She'd just come from Manhattan.

But she couldn't leave her aunt sitting by herself in a sleazy nightclub. She'd phone again, but if she didn't get Aunt Lilith by six-fifteen, she'd go back into the city.

"You'd think she coulda just left her news on the machine," Lily grumbled grabbing a can of soup and a bagel for dinner.

She was still grumbling two hours later on the subway. At least at seven o'clock the place probably wouldn't be too busy. Maybe the owner was one of Aunt Lilith's new students. It was hard to guess what the heck she was thinking. As she neared the small battered doorway of the joint, Lily had even more reservations, but once inside it looked like any other dark, nondescript club. Her nose crinkled at the smell of stale beer.

The music started up when she walked in with some vaguely familiar oldies song. She could hear a guy singing quietly off key as she searched the darkened room for her aunt. There seemed to be only two other couples at tables. Suddenly the singing got louder as the chorus started.

"I keep falling in love with you…"

The Y in you was pronounced like a soft J and Lily's head snapped up to stare at the man on stage. She gaped in shock at Carlos standing there singing to her. He looked mortified as he continued torturing each consecutive note.

Lily stood frozen trying to assimilate the picture. She remembered how adamant he'd been at the resort about not singing. Well, no wonder. The song mercifully ended and she edged up to the stage as Carlos stepped down. As always, he looked perfect with his dark curls just glancing the collar of his beautifully tailored shirt. It was difficult to believe someone so gorgeous could sing so poorly.

"Wow," Lily said uncertainly.

"I know. Very bad, but for you…" He searched her eyes carefully. "I meant it."

"What?"

"I need you. Lily. I cannot live without you."

Lily looked around the club in confusion. *Have I finally lost it?*

"I spoke with your aunt. It is not true what Elena told you. She is an angry, bitter woman."

"But Maria…"

"She thought you meant the bullfight. I knocked a man out for abusing his horse." Carlos rolled his eyes. "I was younger."

Lily grasped the strap of her bag tightly. Could this be real? "Anna said you—"

"Anna Gomez?"

Lily stared at him. "You know my friend?"

"I know of her." He pulled a folded and ripped piece of paper from his inner pocket and showed it to her. There was a small photo of Anna just above an article.

"What is this?"

"I'm sorry. Anna is a journalist sent to New York by *El Primo*. She used you to get information about me."

"Oh." A wave of anger washed over her. How could Anna have lied about being abused? And how much had she written about what Lily had said? "I didn't know when I told her…"

"I know. It doesn't matter now, Lily. Will you come back to me? I've missed you."

She'd daydreamed about Carlos begging her to come back, but now that it was happening she was frozen with fear. She tried to read what was in his eyes. "You mean it?"

"Yes. Are you meaning to keep me in suspense?"

"Oh God, no," Lily answered in a rush as the last vestiges of her anxiety fell away. "I mean, yes, I've missed you, too. No, I don't mean to keep you in suspense. Yes!" Lily threw her arms around his neck and kissed him. His hands trembled at her waist. *Stage fright?*

The DJ let out a whoop and added into the microphone, "Think how much action my man coulda got if he could sing. Who else wants to score a chick?"

Lily glanced at the DJ with embarrassment and pulled Carlos away from the stage. "I take it Aunt Lilith isn't here?"

"No. I tried to have as small an audience as possible. But she does want to hear from you. Now may we leave this place?"

"You don't want to sing some more?" Lily teased.

"No."

It felt so right as he put his arm over her shoulders and walked her outside. She slid her own hand under his light jacket and around his waist. Her insides felt like a mess of Mexican jumping beans. What was she doing? Hadn't she just said she wasn't going to keep breaking up with Carlos?

And yet her aunt had obviously been in on the trick to get her into the nightclub. She must have believed Carlos was being truthful. Lily followed him to the limo that appeared suddenly at the curb beside them. Inside she waited for him to raise the privacy screen so they could kiss again but he merely kept his arm around her shoulders and lightly kissed her forehead. He seemed oddly distracted.

They stopped outside of a stately building on Madison Avenue, and Carlos helped her out of the car. Up the steps, past the uniformed doorman, and into a clean, smell-free elevator. Still he said nothing.

"Um—" Lily started as he led her down the hallway.

Carlos silenced her with a kiss before he pulled out a key and opened the apartment door. It was spacious but, aside from her musical note statue standing beside the fireplace, totally empty. Lily raised her eyebrows in question.

"*Bella*, what do you think?" He appeared apprehensive. "I thought we could decorate it together."

"You mean—" She paused, stunned.

"*Sí*. Our New York apartment. It is close enough so on nice days you can walk to school. And we can turn one room into a studio for you. I will have an office on Lexington."

"But—"

"I will have to work sometimes in Barcelona, but Roberto will be handling most of the business there." Carlos paused and chuckled. "I am doing this badly." He knelt down. "Lily Scott, will you do me the honor of becoming my wife?" He fumbled in his pocket and drew out a small ring box.

Lily stared at him in shock. She looked from his eyes to the solitaire diamond ring in his hands, and up to his eyes again. Was this happening?

"Say something, *mi angelita*." His voice was quiet, but intense.

"Do you love me?" Her voice was also barely above a whisper.

"*Si*. Of course I love you. More than life itself. How could you doubt it?" He looked incredulous.

"Then yes. Yes, I will marry you. Oh God yes!" Lily flung her arms around him as he rose to his feet.

Carlos held her away from him and looked into her eyes. "Do you love me?"

"With all my heart, but I won't ever ask you to sing again." She smiled up at him.

"*Bueno*." Carlos bent over and casually put her over his shoulder in a fireman's hold. "Just pretend you have injured your leg."

"Hey! This isn't the romantic way you carried me when I was injured."

"I know. That was before you insulted my singing voice. And I like the view." Carlos squeezed her butt to illustrate. He carried her into one of the bedrooms. "I took the liberty of buying one piece of furniture for our new home," he informed her as he flopped her back onto a giant bed. Then he jumped on as well, trapping her body beneath his.

"Hmm. Good choice." She kissed him. Her smile faded as he deepened the kiss. "Are you really mine?" she asked quietly when he raised his lips from hers.

"*Si*. And you are stuck with me," Carlos whispered in her ear sending shivers down her spine. "But I do have some bad news. I bought the resort in the Dominican Republic, so we will also have to go there frequently to make sure they are not serving too much food and to check on our horses."

Epilogue

The sound of Aunt Lilith's startled hoot managed to top the rumbling of the espresso machine, the clinking of cutlery and plates, and even the heated discussion in Italian behind the service counter at Café Danté. Lily looked over in alarm, but Carlos had a knowing smile.

"And you say my son let this pass?" Aunt Lilith asked in surprise.

"I believe he said it was all acceptable. He said he had experience with pre-nuptial agreements," Carlos reassured her.

"Uh-huh. And did you read this, Lily?"

"Do I have to?" Lily still didn't want to have to deal with the contract, but had resigned herself.

"Well, I think you should read the conducts clause again. I'm suspicious it might've been altered." Aunt Lilith passed her the papers.

Lily read the page Aunt Lilith indicated and then reread it to see that she understood. She turned an accusing glare at Carlos.

"I have to pose nude in a magazine? Are you nuts?"

"Perhaps a little," Carlos agreed. "If you insist I will take that part out."

"Oh yeah."

"Must I take out the sex in airplane bathrooms clause as well?"

"What?" Lily frantically scanned the document. "That's not in here."

"No. But it would be amusing. None of this matters, *mi amor*. It is merely a formality to keep lawyers in business. Even if you do not sign, my lawyer will keep it on file to keep me honest. The terms are such we cannot afford to ever part."

"Good. No, wait a second, that's not a good reason to stay together."

"Well how about this?" Carlos pulled her to him for a deep kiss, ignoring Lilith's bawdy laugh.

Blushing, Lily cleared her throat after he released her. "That seems like a good reason," she agreed.

"Sweetie," Aunt Lilith interrupted. "That's the best reason in the world."

About the Author

Living in New York and Toronto, Nora Snowdon was a jerk of all trades—one week hawking toys at major toy conventions, the next in a high-end jewelry store pandering to the rich. She worked in the financial market, gambling dens, food service industry and sold shoes. During these years, she also either appeared in or directed over twenty five plays.

Then Nora moved to the West Coast, took up health foods (*dark chocolate and red wine*) and became a *Writer of Elegant Smut*. Her ambition is to become a crazy cat lady and wine hoarder, not necessarily in that order.

You can read more about Nora at *www.norasnowdon.com*.

In the mood for more Crimson Romance? Check out *My Nora* by Holley Trent at *CrimsonRomance.com*.

CPSIA information can be obtained at www.ICGtesting.com
Printed in the USA
LVOW062009270513

335618LV00028B/1272/P